"No you wo

He couldn't help but smile. "Yes I will."

"No you won't."

"I'm going. And that's final."

"No. I'm driving, and you can't come."

At last he'd gotten a reaction from her. The exasperation in her voice was music to his ears. Such a difference from the laid-back woman with the daisy in her hair and a sedate smile, floating around her disorganized shop like an angel in an embroidered blouse.

"Yes, I am."

He was silent, breathing into the receiver and wondering what possessed him to argue like a child with Shannon O'Brien—and enjoy it.

"Why?" she finally demanded. "Why must you go with me?"

"Perhaps I feel like a jaunt in the countryside. I am a foreigner, after all. A stranger in a strange land. Besides, I'm providing the money for a mistake made by *your* employee."

CANDICE SPEARE lives in an old farmhouse in Maryland with Winston the African gray parrot and Jack the dog. You may contact her by visiting her Web site: www.candicemillerspeare.com.

NANCY TOBACK was born and raised in Manhattan and now resides in sunny Florida. Her passion for writing fiction began way back in grammar school. If there's spare time after being wife, mother, grandmother, writer, and avid reader, Nancy is a watercolorist and charcoal artist and enjoys gourmet cooking. You may e-mail her at backtonan@aol.com.

Books by Candice Speare and Nancy Toback

HEARTSONG PRESENTS
HP885—A Hero for Her Heart

Boxed into Love

Candice Speare and Nancy Toback

Heartsong Presents

Authors don't write in a vacuum, and this book is no exception. We'd like to thank John and Diana for Tri-City details, and we want to send a special thanks to Tracy for her help with Benton City information. We also want to mention our wonderful editorial team—JoAnne Simmons, Rachel Overton, and April Frazier. You guys are the best.

A note from the Authors:
We love to hear from our readers! You may correspond with us by writing:

Candice Speare and Nancy Toback
Author Relations
PO Box 721
Uhrichsville, OH 44683

ISBN 978-1-60260-900-6

BOXED INTO LOVE

Our mission is to publish and distribute inspirational products offering exceptional value and biblical encouragement to the masses.

PRINTED IN THE U.S.A.

one

Sleigh bells over the front door of The Quaint Shop jangled, distracting Shannon O'Brien from the task of sorting month-old invoices. As she nudged the door to her office shut with her foot, she decided she preferred the clang of cowbells over the door at her Walla Walla store than this shop in Kennewick. She forced her attention back to her desk. She'd promised herself she'd get this work finished today and didn't need any interruptions. Her clerk, Venus, could take care of customers.

Shannon returned to thumbing through the invoices, but couldn't get her mind to settle. After a quick glance at her guitar leaning against her antique safe, she abandoned her task to find something that required less concentration. Only an hour till closing time, lots to do, and then she had to practice for her guitar lesson with Ray Reed tomorrow night. If only she could better organize her time.

She opened the desk drawer and flipped through three days of mail. Why hadn't she received a new lease from her landlord? Her old lease would expire at the end of the month, and he hadn't returned her calls.

With a long sigh, her dog Truman stretched out next to her. "I fed you," she said. Her own stomach growled in complaint. She'd forgotten to eat lunch, and dinnertime was still a few hours away.

The murmur of voices from the shop drifted through the closed door as Shannon began to punch figures from her checkbook register into the calculator. Truman's ears twitched. She hit the button for the grand total, blinked, and took a sip from a cup of lukewarm herbal tea. The number came up much lower than she'd hoped. How could she manage to keep two stores in two cities when she was earning barely enough to cover her expenses? Somehow she had to make the store more profitable. Betsy Vahn, the woman she left to manage her store in Walla Walla, was doing wonders. Profits from that store were helping keep this one afloat.

The voices were clearer now, and Shannon strained to concentrate over the din. As Venus chattered on and on, the deep rumble of a man's voice followed. Truman sat up, ears cocked toward the door.

Shannon inhaled, breath hissing through her teeth. Not just *any* man—Glen Caldwell, owner of the upper-crust, art deco antique store next to hers. Possibly the most attractive man she'd ever met.

And the most irritating.

The tired floorboards creaked outside her office, followed by a rap at her door. "Shannon, may I come in?"

Oh, that British accent! Truman's tail wagged as fast as her heart thumped. Wasn't twenty-eight too old to have a crush on a foreigner? Shannon motioned for Truman to stay and spun her chair around. "Yes."

The door swung open. Glen hovered in the entry, his head only inches below the door frame, appraising her and her office with one brow raised.

Truman whined.

"I, um, told Mr. Caldwell you were back here," Venus chimed from behind him. Her usual piercing tone was breathy and girlish.

Glen Caldwell had that effect on women with his charming persona and captivating British accent. That's what made listening to his grievances too easy.

"I hope it's okay." Venus peered around Glen, her eyes brimming with curiosity. "I know you said you didn't want to be interrupted, but. . ." She patted down her short, white-blond hair streaked with red and blue, colored to please her new boyfriend, Louis.

"Sure, it's fine." Shannon averted her gaze to the papers on her desk while she tried to put a name to what she felt in Glen's presence.

Magnetism. Glen Caldwell oozed the self-confidence that Shannon felt she'd lost during the last few months.

Shannon pointed to a chair next to the door that hid the stairs to her apartment above the shop. "Come in. Hang up your coat and have a seat." She glanced back at Venus who hovered in the doorway, bouncing from one foot to the other. "Why don't you shut the office door and finish unpacking that Willow Ware."

A frown clouded Venus's eyes, but she sighed and acquiesced, leaving her and Glen alone in her office.

Glen remained standing, staring down at the leather chair beside her desk. "That's a new addition." He stated the obvious. "Well, a *used* new addition."

"Yes, I bought it at an estate sale." The chair didn't look like much, marred by scars and discolorations, but she loved it, and Glen's reaction annoyed her. She pointed. "Sit."

He hesitated.

"It doesn't have bugs." Shannon couldn't help chiding him. "Maybe traces of dog hair. Of course it's not the ritzy stuff you sell, but it's comfortable, dependable, and it happens to be my favorite place to relax now. Take off your coat and sit down. Please."

After he drew a deep breath, Glen hung his black wool coat on a hook on the back of her door and sank into the chair, which put him at eye level with her. The coffee-colored leather sighed as it molded itself around his body. He quickly disguised a look of pleasant surprise before he met her gaze. Perhaps a miracle had happened, and he'd come by to shoot the breeze. She could sit and be mesmerized by the cadence of his speech and—

"This is not a social call," he said.

No, of course not. Shannon adjusted the daisy slipping out

of her hair, leaned back, and noticed Truman had crawled over to lie at Glen's feet. She didn't bother to correct him. He adored Glen, and though she refused to dwell on it, she did, too.

"Can I get you something to drink? I've been practicing making proper English tea, not that I drink a lot of it. I don't want to kill myself with caffeine."

Glen sniffed, a nearly imperceptible gesture he often used to indicate his skepticism. "Thank you, no, though I appreciate the offer." He leaned over to scratch Truman's head.

"Herbal tea, then?"

"No." He cleared his throat and once again settled back into the chair, much to Truman's disappointment.

"So, why are you here?"

"The problem is that your shop has once again been mistaken for mine. This time by the mother of one of my most important clients. How that could happen is quite beyond my comprehension."

Indeed, as he would say. His long list of grievances included her show windows filled with cluttered displays. Her sidewalk sales when she and Venus piled bric-a-brac high on assorted pieces of furniture, which, he claimed, was hazardous to the safety of his clients. Truman's messes in the alley behind the stores, which she often forgot to clean up. The hand-lettered, "garish" sign hanging over the entrance of her store, and her friends and acquaintances—some of whom might be considered unsavory. The thought of her shop being mistaken for his was amusing. What harm could come of it? But for Glen, the mix-up wasn't a mere inconvenience but a personal affront.

"I've explained this to you before, Glen." She took a deep breath, folded her hands in her lap, and made ready to repeat her defense of her store, only with a twist. "When the middle classes of America go antiquing, they're drawn to shops stuffed with junk. Makes them hopeful they'll find something worth thousands that the poor store owner—meaning myself—is too ignorant to identify. That's why they come into my shop first and probably what happened with your client's mother." She spoke with exaggerated patience, very slowly. "Your shop is all retro—glass, steel, wood. That window display of yours is pruned to the point of boring. It discourages the average shopper from entering. In fact, it bleats expensive."

Glen's brows, the same dark brown as his hair, drew together in a frown over eyes that glittered like blue ice through his dark-framed glasses. "Bleats? My window bleats? What precisely does that mean?"

Did she finally have his ear? A sense of satisfaction washed over her. Shannon smiled. "Ever heard a sheep that's stuck? When I was little, we owned one that was so stupid she'd wedge herself between the watering tub and the fence, and since she didn't know how to back up, she'd stand there bleating until someone came to her rescue. It's a sound you can't miss. Like no one can miss your stark, cold window displays filled with art deco stuff that the average customer can't afford to buy."

Glen recovered from her indirect insult with remarkable speed and studied her with a raised brow and slight grin. "I'm not interested in the *average* client. And as much as I find your unique descriptions, er. . .interesting, we need to discuss my client's misplaced spice box."

Shannon's smile slipped. She enjoyed egging him on, if only to keep him around longer, but today he obviously wouldn't be sidetracked. Besides, she still had work to do. "Spice box?" She tilted her head. "Okay. Shoot."

He adjusted his glasses. "The box belongs to Amanda Franklin."

Shannon's hands and stomach clenched at the name of the interior decorator who owned a shop five doors up. "That certainly explains your intense reaction." *And mine,* she thought.

Glen's eyes narrowed. "Some of the wealthiest people in the Tri-Cities and beyond utilize her interior design business, and she's one of my best clients."

"I know that." Shannon held up her hand to stop him. The less she heard about Amanda, the better. The woman disturbed Shannon's equilibrium. "So how am I involved in this? And what do I have to do with her spice box?"

"Well," Glen said, "her mother, Edna Franklin, has senile dementia." His eyes lost their focus like they did when he was about to go off on a tangent. "It's a problem the elderly develop when—"

"I know what it is, Glen." Shannon strummed her fingers on her leg like she was picking guitar strings. "What does that have to do with me?"

He blinked and focused on her again. "Yes, well, Mrs. Franklin made the decision to sell an antique Pennsylvania spice box—part of a valuable collection belonging to Amanda, and she wants it back. In fact, she's threatening legal action, something I see her doing without hesitation. She can be quite unpleasant when she doesn't get her way." He paused and sighed.

Shannon reached for a bag of raw almonds on her desk and held it out to Glen. "I'm well aware of Amanda's unpleasantness from personal experience, but again, what does this have to do with me? I don't understand."

He shook his head at her offer of almonds. "Apparently Mrs. Franklin found my business card on Amanda's desk, called a taxi, and slipped out of the house without her nurse noticing. A call to the taxi company revealed she was dropped off in front of our stores—spice box in hand. She returned several hours later, empty-handed."

"So how do you know she came in here?"

"I don't for certain, but she didn't come into my shop, and I've checked with the other shop owners. If that truly is the case, the poor woman must have confused your shop with mine, influenced, of course, by her dementia."

Shannon fought the brief stab of irritation and reached into the bag for ten almonds—her ration before dinner. "Of course. Anyone of her caliber coming into my shop would have to be demented."

Glen looked sheepish. "Well, you have to admit some of your clientele are—"

"Don't say it." She shoved almonds into her mouth to prevent banging heads with him. She was aware that some of her friends and acquaintances appeared odd, but firmly believed that the outside of a person never told the whole story. Her parents may have had their shortcomings, but they'd taught her to value people for who they were—not for how they looked. Glen wanted The Quaint Shop to be a mirror image of his sterile store, with upscale clientele. But short of a miracle, she would remain herself—a messy perfectionist, a contradiction in personality she'd never understood.

She swallowed. "I'll help you in any way I can."

"Thank you, Shannon."

The sound of her name on his lips usually sent tingles of delight up her spine, but his serious demeanor made her nervous. "Have you seen Amanda's collection of spice boxes?"

"Enough to know that she owns some valuable pieces, but I haven't seen them all. Amanda is eccentric, to say the least. Very touchy about her belongings. However, for this item, she says she'll take no amount of money. Seems this particular box has sentimental value."

"*Sentiment* and *Amanda* are not two words I would ordinarily use in the same sentence." Shannon forced herself to breathe. Amanda was not worth losing her peace.

Glen's lips twitched.

Shannon relaxed and smiled. "Except she might be a tad sentimental when it comes to you. If you could call it that." When Amanda looked at Glen, her gaze often held a predatory gleam. "In fact, her eyes shoot daggers at any woman who approaches you."

Glen's mouth turned down, as if he were considering the validity of her statement.

Shannon laughed and dropped the subject. "So, what does the box look like?"

"It's William and Mary style, made of walnut, pine, and white cedar," he said in a rush. "About eighteen inches tall and seventeen inches wide." Glen demonstrated the approximate size of the box. "I believe its origins are. . ."

Shannon stopped listening and focused on his hands. Strong and capable. Enough to make a girl feel secure. But she had to be reasonable. Dreaming of anything more than a casual acquaintanceship with Glen Caldwell was a waste of time. In his tweed jacket with leather patches on the elbows, he looked exactly like an English lord who should be puttering about in a manor house on a drizzly English moor. Even if he were to take a sudden and miraculous romantic interest in her, their backgrounds were so dissimilar she'd want to challenge him to a duel at dusk within two months.

". . .a woman who matches that description in your shop?" Glen leaned his wiry frame forward as best he could with his body ensconced in the puffy chair.

"Huh?" Shannon realized she'd missed part of what he'd said.

He exhaled. "I asked you if you've seen a woman like that in your shop."

"A woman?" She desperately tried to recall all of what he'd said, but her mind went blank. "I'm sorry. Please tell me again what she looked like."

"You have a habit of daydreaming." Glen sighed. "You do it often."

She could say, *only when I'm around you*, but didn't. In truth, she dreamed all the time, especially about Glen. Instead she shrugged. "Sorry."

"Well, according to Amanda, her mother is tiny, thin,

with sparse white hair and, if you can believe this"—Glen cleared his throat—"she wears flesh-colored trifocals." His lips quirked in a half smile. "Ah, yes, and floral-print dresses."

"*Flesh*-colored trifocals." Shannon laughed. "That could be any number of older women who come in here. I don't recall anyone who matches that description exactly. Well, not the glasses." Shannon thought for a moment. "But I was out this morning. Venus opened the store. She didn't go to school today. Perhaps she remembers something."

"Oh, quite right," Glen said, and his direct gaze made her face warm.

"Venus!" Shannon called out.

"Be right there." Venus used the breathless voice again. The immediacy and clarity of her response told Shannon she'd been close by, probably eavesdropping. So much for the Willow Ware.

Venus burst into the office. "There was somebody with a box like that in here this morning, before Shannon came in. The woman got here really early, like, before I unlocked the door." She stopped and sucked in a deep breath.

Yes, Venus had been listening behind the door.

"Please, do go on." Fingers steepled, Glen leaned forward. "Tell us everything." He used his silky sales voice, the one that had helped him persuade customers to buy thousands of dollars of very expensive antiques.

"Okay, that old lady came in. She was almost creaky, she was so old. She had wrinkles on her wrinkles. Actually, she didn't come in on her own. I mean, the reason she came in is I invited her. I felt sorry for her. She was standing out on the sidewalk, looking cold and lost and. . ."

Venus looked at Glen from under brightly painted eyelids. He nodded and smiled with all of his charm, giving her the full Caldwell treatment. Venus's reaction was immediate. She stood up straighter, a grin lighting her face, making her eyes sparkle.

Like a fire sprinkled with bacon grease, Shannon mused, dismayed by a niggling jab of jealousy. Her teenage clerk was the recipient of the Caldwell charm while Shannon rarely enjoyed that pleasure.

"I told her to come in out of the cold," Venus continued. "I told her she would freeze to death. Her coat didn't look heavy enough—"

"Sweetie," Shannon said, "why don't you get to the point?"

"Oh yeah. Right. So she came in, and I gave her tea. She said she wanted to *dispose* of the box. She wouldn't have peace until she got rid of it. She said something about a secret." Venus frowned. "Strange. I mean, what secret? The box was empty. How weird is that? She reminded me of the ladies in the nursing home where we sang at Christmas last year. Remember, Shannon? Most were old and shaky, but they loved the Christmas carols. Singing at the top of their lungs in those squeaky—"

"I remember." Shannon glanced at Glen. The glint in his eyes reflected her hope that the box was in her shop. She disguised her impatience with Venus under a smile. "Now what about the box?"

"Gee, I felt really sorry for her. She walked bent over, and she looked worried. When I took the box, she was so relieved she almost cried."

Shannon heard Glen's sigh of relief over her own. Though she hadn't spied the spice box amongst the clutter, it had to be in her shop. Maybe this would be a good time to tidy things up—or not. She clasped her hands and turned to face Glen. "It doesn't sound like a case of mistaken identity. Sounds more like the early bird gets the worm." Shannon allowed herself a superior smile. Her shop opened an hour and a half before his.

"Well then, where is it?" Glen snapped, pulling himself to the edge of the slouchy chair, no small feat, and then staring hard at Venus. Her long-winded, convoluted explanations could make the most patient person explode.

Venus bit her lip. Silence filled the room. A mantle clock in the showroom ticked.

"I'll give you three times what you paid for it." Desperation leaked out in Glen's voice, making it low and husky. Decidedly attractive and almost enough to make Shannon daydream again. "Please," he said, "I need that spice box back."

Wow. She would love to hear him say "please kiss me" in that tone. But she had a better chance of performing a classical guitar piece for Ray Reed. Glen asking her for a kiss was the impossible dream, and she was nothing if not pragmatic when it came to love. Shannon returned to the topic at hand. "Venus?"

The girl shifted nervously, looking at the wall, the ceiling, her feet—everywhere but at her or Glen. Shannon's heart sank. Venus had done something with the box and knew they'd be upset.

Venus glanced covertly at Glen. "Yeah, I couldn't get her to take money. Not that I knew what it was worth, so I wouldn't have been able to pay her. And she wouldn't give me her name, so I couldn't do that consignment thing Shannon does." She looked at Shannon and picked at the tight-knit shirt that barely covered her stomach. Was that an earring dangling from her belly button?

Shannon made a mental note to have a discussion with Venus about proper working attire. It would save her one less complaint from Glen on how his classy clientele worried about the "riffraff" who hung around her store.

Glen shifted in the chair and tapped his loafer-clad foot on the floor.

"I didn't know what to do." Venus dragged her fingers through her hair, making her blue tips stand on end. "So I told her to come back for the money. She said she couldn't. She didn't care. She just wanted someone to take the box. She shoved it at me. It was freaky. I got goose pimples all over my body, even on my feet. Then she had me call her a cab. And I did." Venus ended her soliloquy with a dramatic arm flourish.

Glen's foot now kept a rapid rhythm that matched the movement of his fingers on his knees. For someone whose body language indicated agitation, he was acting remarkably patient.

"Venus, honey, where is the box?" Shannon asked the question in the slow, mild tone she used when she tried to obedience-train Truman.

"Right. That's what I'm getting to. Next, this mom and little girl came in. The little girl, around nine, spotted the box and wanted it, so I asked the mom what she'd pay for it. You know, I was, like, bargaining."

Glen stopped moving and groaned.

Tension stiffened Shannon's lips, and she had trouble speaking. "Tell me you didn't sell the box." Amanda already disliked Shannon. This would add fuel to the fire. Amanda's accusations might not stand up in court, but a threat of legal action would force Shannon to hire a lawyer, something for which she had no money. Visions of bankruptcy filled her mind. All her hard work to build her business flushed down the drain.

Venus looked at her feet again as though the leather boots she wore had suddenly caught fire. She mumbled something inaudible.

"What did you say?" Shannon asked. "You need to speak up."

Venus inhaled a gulp of air and glanced up at her with tear-filled eyes, then at Glen.

"I'm really sorry. I sold the spice box."

two

Cold air slapped Glen's face as he emerged from Shannon's shop. He closed the door with a gentleness that belied his agitation. A gentleman and a Christian did not slam his way out of impossible situations. He inhaled, breath hissing through his tight lips with the exertion of maintaining his composure. As he exhaled, streams of white air ballooned toward the steel gray sky, giving veracity to the weather forecaster's prediction of an unusually early snow shower.

How would Amanda Franklin take the news of this bizarre series of events? She'd immediately pounce on Shannon, demanding the return of her property. Perhaps she'd make good on her threat of legal action. As bullheaded as Shannon could be, she was no match for Amanda, even though a lawsuit like this had no teeth.

Glen hunched his shoulders against the cold and picked his way around the battered benches and scarred chairs and tables placed in front of Shannon's shop for her sidewalk sale. The furniture held everything, from old kitchen utensils to Depression glass. "Clutter," he mumbled and examined his window display. Shannon's comments wouldn't leave him alone. Was his window too stark? Too cold? *Bleating* expensive?

Glen shook his head. What did Shannon O'Brien know about aesthetics? Nothing, if her front windows were any example. And the furniture she placed at least once a week on her sidewalk was a hazard, leaving little room for pedestrians—a complaint he'd given up lodging with her. Had she ever heeded his advice? No. Other store owners had complained as well, Amanda in particular.

Ah well, no matter how often Shannon ignored him, he was persistent if nothing else. He was determined to find a way to get the flower child next door to clean up her shop—for her own good.

The chill November wind penetrated his wool coat as he reached his shop. Would he ever get used to the winds that blew year-round across the desert of the Tri-Cities? Who would have thought there could be such a dichotomy of climate in one state? Rain in one corner and desert in the other. He shivered and pushed open the door, welcomed by delicate tinkles from silver chimes. Not sleigh bells like Shannon's.

Charlie Wyatt, his clerk, greeted him with a smile. "You're back, Mr. Caldwell."

"Yes." Glen glanced at the teen's khakis and black polo shirt, comparing him with Venus and her inappropriate attire. The conservative young man would never play owner at Caldwell Antiques the way Venus had in Shannon's shop.

"You were next door for a while." Charlie frowned as if to say, *What happened this time?*

Glen met his wary gaze. "Yes, why do you say that?"

Charlie shrugged. "Venus and I have some classes together at CBC."

"That's the community college?" Glen asked.

Charlie nodded. "Columbia Basin."

"I see." But Glen didn't really see why that fact bore mentioning. "Did I get any calls?"

Charlie jumped to attention. "Oh, yes. Sorry. Four calls. One from Mike Carroll about that possible expansion of your store. Says he'll see you after work Friday at that new French restaurant in Richland. They have a piano player, which he knows you'll enjoy. The other three calls were from Amanda Franklin. She wanted to know if you found the spice box. And she said something about that petition again." Charlie's narrow glance told him he hadn't yet figured out the relationship between Amanda and Glen.

Glen nodded. "Thank you." He hadn't figured out his relationship with her either. Her purchases brought in 30 percent of his income. He had no choice but to cater to her eccentricities while avoiding her obvious attempts to change their relationship from business to personal. Lately Amanda was obsessed with collecting signatures for a petition about renewing storefronts. She cajoled Glen into signing it early on, and he hadn't paid much attention to what it said. He just added his signature so she'd go away and leave him alone. She told him she planned to present the signatures to Mike, the landlord. Glen hoped that perhaps renewing the storefronts would encourage Shannon to clean up her act.

Glen took the written messages from Charlie. Mike Carroll's message was a follow-up to a conversation they'd had a week ago. "I wonder if the gift shop next door is going out of business. Have you heard anything, Charlie?"

"No, sir."

"Hmm, must be if Mike's offering me more space." Joe, the gift shop owner, had implied that business hadn't been good recently.

Charlie cleared his throat. "Venus texted me and told me about the spice box."

Glen looked over his glasses at the teenager. "Did she?" Odd that Venus would text Charlie. He couldn't imagine the two being friends, but what did he know about kids?

"Yes. She feels really bad about it."

"As well she should. What she did was irresponsible."

"She said it must be worth a lot if everyone is so worried about getting it back."

"I'm sure it is, but it may be more the sentimental value." Even as Glen said the words, he remembered Shannon's comment. Amanda was anything but sentimental.

Charlie's phone vibrated in his pocket, and he snatched it out and opened it to read a text message. When he was done,

Glen eyed him. "I hope you don't spend all your time on your cell phone when I'm out."

"No, Venus is just upset, that's all." Charlie looked as if he wanted to defend Venus's honor, but didn't follow through. Wise of him. Glen wasn't in the mood to be delicate.

He strode through the store, soothing himself by admiring the clean lines of the furniture he had for sale, all made from smooth wood, metal, and glass. He reached his office in the back, dropped into his chair, and rested his elbows on the spotless top of the desk. How did Shannon find anything on her cluttered desktop? He leaned back, tucked his hands behind his head, and closed his eyes. He had to figure out a way to pacify Amanda and save Shannon from her wrath. Beneath Shannon's harebrained, carefree exterior, he had a hunch she worried a great deal about everything. And her friends—many of them outcasts and oddballs.

So why did thoughts of the outwardly unflappable Shannon keep him up nights? Glen sat forward and caught a flash of movement in the back alleyway behind their stores. "Shannon," he whispered. She sat on an old painted bench she'd placed there, chatting with Truman while stroking his massive head. She'd found the dog along the side of the road and immediately gone on a mission to locate his owner. When she couldn't, she adopted him. The dog was quite possibly the ugliest he'd ever seen.

Glen stood and positioned himself between two tall file cabinets where she couldn't see him. Spying! That's what he'd resorted to. For the past year he'd tried valiantly to ignore her charm and whimsical colloquialisms. To close his eyes to the beauty of her fresh-scrubbed, heart-shaped face and hazel eyes that brimmed with warmth and wonder.

Shannon rose, straightened her wool poncho, then adjusted her peasant skirt and tugged at her embroidered, bell-sleeved blouse. Glen grimaced. He had an eye for fashion, a necessity in dealing with his type of clientele, and Shannon's style made her look like a throwback from the sixties. Hair in a gold-streaked plait reached the middle of her back and enhanced the look. Her skirt swirled as she walked in the direction of her store. He could almost see her hair loose and windblown, sparkling in the—

Whoa, Glen! He had to stop right there. He was mad for even entertaining the thought. The woman was the most annoying creature he'd ever met—this side of the Atlantic or the other. And then there was that crazy dog of hers.

Glen sat at his desk, opened the Johnson folder, and scanned the invoices. The order Amanda had placed for her client was near completion, but what if he didn't get that box back to her? And Shannon. . .would Amanda retaliate?

The phone rang. A welcomed distraction. Glen promptly swiped it off its cradle without checking caller ID. "Good afternoon, Caldwell Antiques. How may I help you?"

"Glen? This is Shannon."

Odd that she would call just as he was thinking about her. Perhaps he thought of her too often. "Hello, Shannon. What can I do for you?"

"I'd say it's more what I can do for you." She laughed.

His shoulders stiffened. "And what might that be?"

"Weeelll," she began, taking her sweet time about it. "I reached the lady who bought the box. You know? The spice box you're looking for? The one Amanda is frothing at the mouth like a rabid dog to have back?"

Another colloquialism that exactly suited the situation. He couldn't help but grin. Shannon was baiting him, and he would avoid the hook. "Yes?"

"It seems the little girl took the box with her to a friend's house for a sleepover. At least that's what Lucy Jennings, the girl's mother, told me."

"And?" He refused to give in.

"And? You want to know the rest, do you?"

Glen heard laughter in her voice and sat back, waiting

patiently for more. He enjoyed this game.

"Okay, I'll have mercy on you. The little girl will return tomorrow morning. I'll run over to their house then and buy back the box. They live in Benton City." She paused. "A place I'm all too familiar with." She said the words so softly, he almost missed them. "Anyway, Lucy Jennings has agreed to our very generous offer of five times what she paid for it."

"Wh–what?" Glen jolted forward in his chair. "I said *three* times the price, not five."

"Glen, the mom seemed hesitant to take the box from her daughter. I had to up the price and beg her to have mercy on me. Of course, I'll pay you back the fifty dollars Venus got for it."

"Fifty? That box is worth at least four hundred."

"How would Venus have known that? Anyway, this means I saved you over a hundred dollars, right?"

"A hundred dollars? What are you talking about? That doesn't make sense at all. I hope that isn't how you keep your books. You'll go bankrupt." Dismissing her skewed logic, he considered the offer. What choice did he have? "Fine," he said, "and I'll go with you to pick up the box." Glen shook his head. His offer had *big mistake* written all over it.

Shannon was silent, a rare occurrence. Glen paced his office, gratified that he'd found a way to render her mute.

"No you won't," she finally said.

He couldn't help but smile. "Yes I will."

"No you won't."

"I'm going. And that's final."

"No. I'm driving, and you can't come."

At last he'd gotten a reaction from her. The exasperation in her voice was music to his ears. Such a difference from the laid-back woman with the daisy in her hair and a sedate smile, floating around her disorganized shop like an angel in an embroidered blouse.

"Yes, I am."

He was silent, breathing into the receiver and wondering what possessed him to argue like a child with Shannon O'Brien—and enjoy it.

"Why?" she finally demanded. "Why must you go with me?"

"Perhaps I feel like a jaunt in the countryside. I am a foreigner, after all. A stranger in a strange land. Besides, I'm providing the money for a mistake made by *your* employee."

"Oh, please. You've lived in this country long enough now. And don't go blaming Venus. She meant well. If Amanda had taken better care of her belongings—and her mom—this would've never happened."

"Okay, all right." Glen blew out a breath. My, she was defensive of her friends. "So I'll see you tomorrow?"

Shannon sighed, long and loud. "I'm leaving at seven. That's seven in the morning. That's early, and you hate early. I'll see you then. . .Old Chap." She chuckled and hung up.

Grinning, Glen replaced the receiver, relishing his minor victory.

"That went well." Of course he was now obligated to be in Shannon's rattletrap truck for the drive to Benton City. His smile faded. What if she drove in the haphazard way she tended her shop? Worse, he would be in close quarters with a woman who drove him crazy in too many ways. Avoiding her was easier than trying to figure out his feelings. His victory didn't look good when viewed in that light. In fact, the whole thing was a bad idea. A horrible idea. What had he done?

But perhaps he could put the drive to good use and try to convince her to clean up her eyesore of a shop.

The door chimes sounded, and Glen peered through the glass walls of his office. Amanda Franklin stood at the counter. Charlie turned, looked beseechingly at Glen, and motioned for him to come to the rescue.

Glen strode from his office into the shop area. "Amanda, hello."

She turned her impeccably made-up face toward him.

Her black hair bounced in loose curls over her shoulders. A silk blouse, expensive jeans, and a wool jacket were snug on her model-thin figure that Glen was sure she achieved with constant diet and exercise. She had looks, money, and a certain vibrancy and confidence that many men would find enticing. Not Glen. She was also abrasive and self-consumed. Besides, she had no curves like Shannon.

"Hello, Glen, have you located the box?" Long fingers tipped with perfectly manicured nails grasped a designer purse that had to cost at least a thousand dollars.

Why did the box deserve so much attention? It wasn't for its monetary value. "I discovered that your mother left the box with my colleague next door."

"Shannon?" Amanda hefted her purse strap on her shoulder and took a step toward the door. "I'm going to get it."

Glen put his hand on her arm. "Unfortunately, it was sold, and no wonder. I'm sure it was exquisite."

He felt the tension in her arm muscle as she drew herself up to full height. "Please tell me you didn't just say, 'It was sold'?"

"I'm afraid so, but we intend—"

"How could that woman be so ignorant?"

Glen took a deep breath. "Shannon didn't sell the box. Her employee did."

"You mean that blue-haired, skinny creature that looks like she belongs in a freak show?"

Charlie squared his shoulders and opened his mouth, but Glen caught his eye and shook his head. Fortunately, Amanda was too enraged to notice the exchange.

"I'm going over there right now."

"Wait, please. We can work this out."

"I won't be charmed, Glen. I want the box back."

"I know that. We've located the buyer in Benton City. We're going there tomorrow to get it."

Amanda clutched her purse so tightly, her knuckles turned

white. "Who's the buyer?" Her lips thinned. "I'll attend to the matter myself."

"How long have you known me, Amanda? Long enough to know I keep my word." Glen looked her in the eye, smiled, and took her hand. "The buyer is Shannon's customer, and even if I did know the name, the information is confidential. But I promise I'll get that box back to you."

The emotion in Amanda's eyes was a curious mixture of fear, irritation, and attraction to him. Her lips moved as she struggled to speak—probably deciding between demanding her way or acceptance of his word. She scanned him head to toe. "Your colleague next door has been nothing but trouble, Glen. She and her ilk stand out like sore thumbs in this neighborhood. You really should make it your business to deal with her."

Glen swallowed his desire to rally in Shannon's defense. "She means well. I'm sure—"

"You're truly chivalrous, Glen." Some of the fire left her eyes. "That's certainly admirable, but she doesn't belong here. My Renew Our Storefronts idea will improve the neighborhood. Shannon's signature is not on my petition, by the way."

Glen didn't miss her implication that the remedy would have a negative impact on Shannon, and he didn't know how to counteract that. "She will come around. Straighten things up. I'm certain of that."

She drew a long, dramatic sigh, and her face hardened. "I plan a heart-to-heart with Mike Carroll when I present my petition to him." Amanda narrowed her eyes as if in challenge. "I will *make* him remedy the situation." She sighed, headed for the door, then turned. "I've done business with you for the past five years. I wouldn't want to have to stop now. . . ." She let her voice trail off, whirled on her heel, and exited his shop.

Glen blew out a breath and wondered why Amanda disliked Shannon so. The reason couldn't possibly be just the condition of Shannon's store. He glanced at his watch and turned to Charlie who had listened with interest to the conversation. "I'm sorry you had to be privy to that exchange."

"Are you kidding, Mr. Caldwell?" Charlie snorted. "I'm learning more from you than in any classroom. You're a real communicator. Smooth talking."

Is that what he was? A smooth talker? Not at all flattering. All he meant to do was restore peace and tranquility—and save Shannon's hide.

Sudden fatigue hit. "It's half past five. Why don't we close up shop? I don't think we'll get any more customers on this blustery evening."

Charlie's eyes widened, and he fairly ran to lock the front door.

With the CLOSED sign in the window, Glen poked around in the cash register. "Go on, Charlie. I'll see you tomorrow." He recalled he would be out. "Wait a minute, I forgot. I'm going with Shannon tomorrow morning to find that box. Take a spare key home so you can open the shop if for some reason I'm not back when you arrive after school." Glen removed a key from the cash register drawer and held it out to him.

"You're going with Shannon O'Brien?" Charlie stared, eyes round with disbelief. "Out? Together?"

Glen frowned. Why did people tend to imagine nonexistent liaisons in the simplest actions? "Charlie, listen to me. We are going to get the spice box. It's *not* a date. Okay?"

"Okay." Charlie grinned, took the key, and left in haste.

Glen sighed. That was a quick getaway.

&

Shannon stared at the calendar above the counter. Venus walked up behind her. "Is something wrong?"

"No," Shannon said. "Well, just a little. I give my testimony at church on Sunday morning, and I'm already nervous."

"I'll come to support you for sure," Venus said.

Shannon smiled at her gratefully. "Thank you. That would really help me. Hey, it's slow today. I'm going to unpack a couple of boxes. You can leave if you'd like. And thank you for your help pulling the sidewalk sale stuff inside." She headed to the storeroom, then stopped. "Have you seen that pair of antique salt and pepper shakers? The dog and the cat? Did someone buy them?"

Venus blinked. "They aren't here?"

"No. That's odd." Shannon began walking again and gave her helper a backhanded wave. "No matter. They'll turn up. Just lock up when you go. And make sure you have your key in case for some reason I'm not here when you come in after classes tomorrow. I'm going to pick up that spice box."

"Do you have a guitar lesson tonight or tomorrow night?" Venus asked.

"Tomorrow night, and I haven't done much practicing. Fortunately Ray is patient."

"Has he kissed you?"

"What?" Shannon skidded to another stop and turned to face Venus. "Ray? Of course not! He's like a brother."

"Are you sure? He's nice-looking in a dark way, like Heathcliff in a leather jacket."

Shannon laughed at Venus's description of the hero from *Wuthering Heights*. "I'm positive." She headed once again to the storeroom, and Venus followed closely on her heels like Truman always did. Which reminded her. "Where's the dog?"

"In the alley on his leash."

"Oh good. Thanks for letting him out. He loves the cold. I sometimes wonder if he really is part wolf."

"Yeah, me, too," Venus said without humor. "Do you think the old lady was crazy?"

"I don't like to use that word *crazy* when it comes to anyone." Shannon heaved a cardboard box filled with antique books onto a table. "Everyone has their own reality." She pulled the top open. The distinctive, dusty smell of old paper wafted up to her nose. She ran her hands gently over the frayed bindings, then looked at Venus. "We need to get that box back before Amanda hires a lawyer and claims we took advantage of her elderly mother."

Venus shifted from foot to foot. "I'm really sorry I caused this problem."

Shannon shrugged. "It's okay. Now you know, and next time you won't take things into your own hands. You're not experienced enough yet. But I'm willing to teach you this business if you've got the passion." She dusted off her hands and glanced at the repentant young woman. "The problem is, I'm suffering for your mistake. I have to drive to Benton City with *Glen* to get that box."

Venus's eyes grew wide. "Wow. I'm sorry. I know how you feel about Benton City. Is that why you're suffering? Or is it—"

"Imagine being in an enclosed space like my truck with the man who is so critical of my store." Shannon clamped her mouth shut. She was about to say Glen was critical of her, too, but he'd never treated her with disdain—only as if she were a strange creature from another planet.

"I wouldn't mind being in a car with him." Venus wore a dreamy smile. "He's really good-looking."

Shannon blinked. So, Venus did think Glen was attractive. "What about his British stiff upper lip?"

"Stiff lip?" Venus frowned. "No. He's not stiff. Not at all." She looked wistful. "More like those well-bred, gentlemanly types I see in old movies. Don't you just love when he says things like 'perhaps' and 'quite'?" She giggled and turned to go. "Well, see you tomorrow afternoon."

Shannon folded her arms on the edge of the box and rested her chin on top. Glen was certainly good-looking in a royal sort of way, with tousled brown hair and crystal blue eyes.

Stop there, Shannon. The man was so her opposite. She could only imagine what his family was like. Probably upper-crust breeding all the way.

She shook her head as if it would help clear her mind of the antique dealer next door, then reached into the box. Better to think about books. Safer on the emotions.

&

Glen exited the back of his store, locked up, and tossed a bag of trash into the rusted receptacle. He heard noises, turned, and saw Charlie walking toward him, head down.

"What are you still doing here, Charlie? You left a good twenty minutes ago."

"Don't look now, Mr. Caldwell, but Venus is at the end of the alley with that boyfriend of hers, Louis."

Glen couldn't help but look. Venus stood beside a red sports car, smiling up at the fellow. "My, he's stocky. Like a wrestler. Where did she meet him?"

"Through some friends at community college. He doesn't attend, just sometimes hangs around." Charlie's expression darkened. "He's got money and spends it on her."

The teen sounded envious. "Money isn't everything," Glen said.

"Yeah, well, it means a nice car and lots of money to spend on a girl. I don't have that kind of extra money. I'm just scraping by."

Glen nodded his understanding. Charlie lived alone with his mother, and they struggled. Charlie had to pay for college as well as contribute to household expenses.

"I wish she'd break up with him. I really don't like him."

Glen blinked, but kept his surprise to himself. Until this afternoon he hadn't been aware that Charlie and Venus knew each other. In fact, he didn't know much about the kids at all. He should've taken the time. Charlie continued to stare toward the end of the alley, his mouth quirked to one side, blinking rapidly. Were those tears in his eyes?

Truth dawned, and Glen looked away from him. Charlie was in love with Venus. How odd. Charlie was a good boy, worked hard in school and on the job. Venus was, well,

Venus. An airhead. A bit like Shannon. Glen patted Charlie's shoulder. "Don't worry. God has a way of working these things out. You just concentrate on your education." Great. A cliché response with nothing of real meaning to console the teen. Still, only the young would be so naive as to think a relationship of such opposites could work.

Charlie offered a polite smile and walked away, and an eruption of noise sent a shudder through Glen. He spun around. Ray Reed turned his motorcycle into the alley, roared past Venus and Louis, at the last minute swerved past Glen, and stopped at the back of Shannon's store. Her infamous guitar teacher whipped off his helmet and nodded hello.

You nearly ran me down, was on the tip of Glen's tongue, but Shannon emerged from the back door of her shop and gave Reed a welcoming hug, a distraction that rendered Glen tongue-tied. She then looked over Reed's shoulder, and her eyes widened. "Oh, Glen. I didn't see you."

Neither had Ray when he'd almost run over him.

"Good day." Glen turned and headed toward his car. Here he was, trying to protect Shannon from Amanda, but Shannon continued to befriend questionable people. Ray was a recent addition to her stable of strays—except that a stray wouldn't be able to afford a Harley like Reed's.

Glen sat behind the wheel of his car, staring at the back of The Quaint Shop. Shannon lived above her store. Who was he besides her guitar teacher, and why'd she hug him like that? Would she invite him upstairs for dinner after her lesson?

Glen threw the gearshift into DRIVE. She was a magnet for oddballs and ne'er-do-wells. None of his business, except that he wanted to help the flower child who refused to help herself.

three

Early on Wednesday morning, Glen stepped out of his car and groaned. Shannon was right. He was not a morning person. Especially not a wintry morning person. The cold, dry desert wind cut through his jacket like a sharp blade. As he tramped toward Shannon, he adjusted his foggy eyeglasses and tried to wipe the painful scowl off his face. Why give her the satisfaction?

"It's quite brisk this morning, isn't it?" Shannon stood beside her rusted truck, smirking.

She was baiting him again. "*Brisk* is not the word I'd use to describe it. *Glacial*, *arctic*, or *frigid* are more apropos. But. . ." Glen released his grip on the lapels of his coat and looked up. "Refreshing, isn't it?"

As he drew closer to her truck, it appeared that the seat was stuffed with something large. He blinked, pulled off his glasses, and took a step back. *Oh, fantastic!*

A pair of bright eyes stared at him through the window. Truman's massive, furry body wriggled in anticipation of his approach.

"Hope you don't mind Truman is coming." Shannon hopped into the truck and slammed the door.

And my presence on this trip was my idea. I am a complete idiot. Glen opened the truck door and dove in.

Truman seized the opportunity to stick his cold nose in his neck, wetting his ear with a doggy kiss. Glen shuddered and pulled a handkerchief from his pocket.

"Sorry." Shannon laughed as she started the engine. "He adores you, and he's happy you're going with us. I told him on the way here, and he got all excited."

Not only does she take her dog to therapy, she talks to him and thinks he's listening. "I thought wolves were supposed to be vicious and unfriendly." Glen pushed away the dog's persistent, hairy muzzle.

"Oh, come on, Truman's not really part wolf. I'm sure that vet was exaggerating." Shannon pulled away from the curb and started up the street at a sedate pace. "I'm sorry I ever shared that story with you." Her smile broadened.

Shannon began humming, and the dog tilted his head and stared at Glen, who in turn pressed himself against the passenger door. Even so, Truman's body was glued to his.

Glen stared out the window. It was too early and too cold to be out, let alone in a truck with a loony woman and her overly enthusiastic, part-wolf attack dog. There had been no time for a proper cup of tea or relaxed Bible reading—something he enjoyed every morning. On the positive side, at least the dog's body offered some warmth.

Shannon stopped humming and looked at him. "Glen?"

He grunted and turned his head toward her.

"I brought a thermos of tea for you." Shannon pulled out a steel canister from behind the seat, reached around Truman, and handed it to Glen with a pleased expression.

Shannon's ever-present herbal tea. Great. "Er, thank you."

He had no choice. She'd been kind enough to make it for him; now he'd do his utmost to pretend to enjoy it.

"I added sugar and cream." Shannon glanced at him with those hazel eyes that seemed to see right through him.

"In herbal tea?" What a horrific combination.

She laughed, a pleasing and contagious sound. "Not herbal tea, Glen. This is English tea. And I made it just the way you like it."

"How do you know what I take in my tea?" Glen glanced at her suspiciously, then unscrewed the lid and poured some into the plastic top. Proper English tea should be steeped in a porcelain teapot. Not stainless steel. Well, at least it would be hot.

"First off, I'm a woman, which makes me hyperobservant. Women see lots of things men miss." She pulled onto the interstate. "Also—and only my closest friends know this— I'm a student of body language."

Glen laughed. "I guess that means I'm one of your closest friends because I knew that already. You've mentioned it before." Body language, indeed. He inhaled deeply. Perhaps this trip would not be a wash after all. He needed a refresher course on why he should not be attracted to the messiest store owner in town. Shannon, with her Bohemian lifestyle, could not possibly be the woman for him.

Satisfied with his conclusion, Glen settled back in his seat. The steam drifting from the plastic cup smelled marvelous. He must be quite desperate for tea. Blowing gently on the liquid, he lifted it to his lips. The first sip made him blink. There had to be some mistake. The tea tasted almost as good as his own. He took another sip. No mistake.

"You're surprised."

He studied Shannon's profile. Light freckles dusted her nose and cheeks, and a small daisy was tucked behind her ear. Wisps of hair escaped the customary braid. The desire to reach over and stroke them back into place came over him so suddenly that he almost dropped the cup. He had to stop this nonsense. He'd do well to remember the last twelve months of owning a shop next to hers. Frustrating months filled with disputes he could never win against Shannon's illogical logic. The piles Wolf-dog left in the back alley that she "forgot" to clean up. Her sidewalk sales—a lawsuit waiting to happen. But then there were all the times she made him laugh and think. The times she surprised him. Like right now.

She blushed. "Quit staring. I am capable of doing *some* things right."

"Indeed." Glen took another sip. "Thank you. It's excellent."

Silver slivers of snow began to fall as the tea warmed his chest. She pushed a button on the dash. The sounds of

Mozart from a surprisingly good stereo filled the vehicle. Thank heavens it wasn't the strange music that usually came from her store—or her noisy attempts at learning guitar from Mr. Leather Jacket—Ray Reed.

"Nice sound," he murmured.

"Ray brought the stereo to me and helped me install it. He said he got it from a friend in town."

Ray Reed again. "He certainly does a lot for you."

"He's like family," she said, smiling.

Family. Glen shoved Mr. Leather Jacket from his mind and chose to daydream about a warm, misty English countryside. He imagined walking around a small pond where frogs croaked in peaceful syncopation. The croaking grew louder. Glen's pleasant interlude came to an abrupt end when he realized what he heard wasn't frogs at all. It was gagging.

"Wh–what's that?"

"Truman." Shannon sighed and cut the dog a sympathetic look. "Oh, my poor baby."

"I know it's the dog," Glen snapped. "What is he doing?"

"He's about to lose his breakfast. I need to pull over."

"Lose his breakfast?" Glen moved forward in his seat, as far away from Wolf-dog as space would permit. "That's revolting. Does he do this often?"

"There's an exit right here," she mumbled.

"Please do it quickly," Glen murmured. The dog was gagging in a rhythmic way that left no doubt time was running short.

Shannon whipped the car right onto an exit ramp and pulled over on the shoulder.

Glen shook his head. "Do you mean to tell me the dog is going to retch here? On the side of the exit ramp?"

"*Hurl,* as Venus would say. Would you rather he do it in your lap?" Shannon flung open her door. As if rehearsed, Truman hopped out, ran to the grass, and deposited the contents of his stomach in the dramatic, unpleasant way dogs do.

Glen felt as if the tea in his stomach curdled. He looked

away but couldn't eliminate the sound from reaching his ears. He concentrated on deep breathing until the dreadful interval finally ended, and he heard Shannon murmuring to the dog. Venturing a look, he saw her caress Truman's head as he stood on wobbly legs, sides heaving.

"That's better, isn't it, Truman?" The dog wagged its hairy tail. And just like that, the incident was over. Shannon fetched a bottle of water and a dish from a bag behind the backseat and offered the dog a drink.

"Should you do that?" Glen's stomach tightened. Suppose it all started again ten miles up the road?

"It's just a sip." Shannon had already taken the bowl from Truman. "The whole thing was my fault. He slurped too much water on top of his breakfast. He's got a sensitive stomach, especially in a car."

Great. The dog had a sensitive stomach. He was trapped in a vehicle with a dog liable to retch at any time, and it had been his idea to come along. It was like a British comedy of errors.

"Are you ready now?" Shannon cooed, as if he were a child.

"I'm more than ready to get on with this," he grumbled.

"I'm not talking to you. I'm talking to the dog."

Truman's answer came in the form of hopping back into the truck. Glen tried to move away, but Truman landed an enthusiastic lick on his cheek.

"Dreadful," Glen groaned, not even bothering with the handkerchief as he leaned forward to avoid another smooch from the wolf.

"Truman, sit," Shannon said. The dog obeyed, perching happily between them and once again leaning against the back of the seat to stare at Glen.

"I'm sorry, Glen. That was unpleasant for me, and I'm used to it. I'll see that he doesn't drink so much on top of breakfast next time."

There won't be a next time, Glen thought.

❧

Farther down the highway, Shannon chanced a glance at Glen. He hadn't moved. Eyes closed, he held the empty cup in very still hands.

"You look sort of greenish. Why don't you have more tea?"

"I'm fine. I don't want more." He sounded like a petulant child.

"You need more. It'll make you feel better. Don't make me stop this vehicle." She used her dog-training voice, then grinned at his stunned expression. "Do it, please."

He picked up the thermos without further argument, much to her surprise.

"Anybody ever tell you you're pushy?" Glen elbowed Truman's nose away, poured the tea, and placed the thermos back on the floor. "And stubborn?"

"That's the pot calling the kettle black." She paused and sighed. "Maybe it's a survival technique."

He stared at her. "What do you mean by that?"

She wasn't about to reveal her past to this pampered English gentleman. She had never expected pity from anybody and wouldn't start mining for it now. She shrugged. "It's not important."

As they entered the outskirts of Benton City, Shannon felt around in her purse for the directions to the Jennings' house, keeping one hand on the wheel. Unable to locate the paper, she looked down into her handbag.

Glen cleared his throat. "I'm not comfortable when the driver of a vehicle I'm riding in isn't looking through the windscreen."

"I can't find my directions. The piece of paper wasn't on my desk where I left it, so I assumed I'd shoved it into my purse." Shannon tossed the bag in his lap. "Would you mind looking for it?"

Truman sat up and jabbed his nose inside the bag. Glen pushed away his snout and stared inside. "In *here*?"

"Yes, in *there*." Shannon caught a glimpse of the Kleenex and pieces of paper that overflowed the zippered opening. She had meant to clean it out, but forgot.

Holding it open with the tips of his fingers, he peered inside. "This is a bit like maneuvering around your store."

"I'm not laughing," she said.

"Will I get hurt if I stick my hand inside? I'm not sure when I had my last tetanus shot."

"Ha-ha. Very funny, Glen. It's not that bad."

"You're quite mistaken." With a slight grin, he dangled a lint-covered Life Saver in front of her face. "Do you have plans for this?"

"I'm ignoring your snide comments. The directions are on a purple piece of paper with black writing." Glen's criticism disturbed her balance despite his smile. Recently, what he thought of her had become important. When had that changed? Perhaps when she'd talked herself into believing he looked at her in a certain way. Held her gaze longer than what was required for polite conversation. Pathetic! Shannon dismissed her fantasies and drew deep, calming breaths.

One by one, with dramatic flourishes, he pulled all the contents from her purse onto his lap. Truman's head bobbed with each of Glen's movements. Finally Glen stared around the dog at her.

"What?" Shannon frowned.

"I found two pieces of gum—unwrapped. A package of crushed saltines, unopened. One Life Saver, mentioned previously. Innumerable tissues—used or new, I'm unable to determine. One torn leather wallet stuffed with everything *except* a piece of purple paper. A date book complete with addresses and phone numbers, but no purple paper. Two sets of keys, three dog biscuits, assorted hair ties, three tubes of lipstick—one missing its top, and—"

"All right!" Shannon clenched the steering wheel. "You've made your point. My purse is a mess, and yours—if you carried one—would be as pristine as that shop of yours. Anyone can see you're nearly perfect. I'm sure you have blue blood flowing through your English-bred veins."

"Actually, my family comes from—"

"I don't really care right now, Glen."

"Sorry. Still, that doesn't change the fact that the directions are nowhere to be found."

She glanced at him. "Stop smirking."

"What do you mean?"

"And stop acting superior."

Glen arched an eyebrow. "Me?"

Shannon bit back a grin. "Please put the stuff back in my purse. The last place I recall seeing that paper was on my desk. I guess I left it there. Now I'll have to remember how to find this house."

"Shall I tidy your bag up a bit while I'm putting all these things away?" Glen asked. "I'm sure I'll have ample time, given that you'll have to remember your way."

With a sidelong glance, Shannon cleared her throat. "Whatever floats your boat. Tidy away if you must. But no worries. My memory is quite impressive. We'll be there in a jiffy." She smiled. No need to exaggerate. Excellent recall was one of her strong points.

With only one wrong turn, she found the Jennings' house. It stood solitary with lots of tall trees growing in the yard, thanks to irrigation. The tan-sided one-story rancher blended into the tans and browns of the surrounding treeless hills. In the driveway, a minivan was parked next to a Benton County Sheriff's Office patrol car. As she pulled up behind them, ugly memories surged to the surface of her mind.

"Are you sure you have the right house?" Glen pushed his glasses up the bridge of his aquiline nose.

Shannon looked away from his handsome face. *Lord, please don't let this be an embarrassment to me.* "Yes, I am. Told you

I had good recall." She looked at the cars again. "Maybe the man of the house is part of the sheriff's department."

"We'll find out soon enough." Glen opened his door and got out.

Truman whined, and Shannon turned her head to tell him to behave while she was gone. She heard her door open and swiveled around. Glen stood there, hand extended, waiting for her to get out. She was baffled as to what to do next.

"I *am* a gentleman, no matter what else you think of me." He smiled—a brilliant, flash-of-teeth smile.

Mute, Shannon glanced from his face to his outstretched hand. As she reached out, a flood of bewildering emotions shut down her brain and made her breathing erratic. Finally, she knew what it felt like to touch his hands. Wonderful and strong, just as she'd imagined. Her only rational thought was to ask herself why the notion of holding Glen's hand made her feel sorry for herself. The memory came back in a flash. She was the wallflower at the high school dance, and the prom king, a sweet, good-looking guy, took pity on her and asked her to dance. Nice of him, but a little humiliating because everyone knew what he was doing.

Glen's hand closed around hers, and warmth coursed through her. She met his gaze, held her breath. She didn't like what was happening to her heart, and just as bad, now she had to face one of Benton County's finest. She prayed he or she wasn't someone she knew.

❧

Glen didn't know what to think. Shannon's expression was that of someone who had witnessed an accident. Had his innocent gesture of helping her out of the car made her uncomfortable? Or did she dislike him that much? Glen glanced over his shoulder. She lagged a good distance behind him, gaze glued to the patrol car. No, Shannon didn't dislike him. He knew that. Something else was going on.

A deputy with graying hair walked out of the house, saw

them, and crossed the yard with long strides. Glen nodded a greeting.

"Can I help you?" The uniformed man tilted his head.

"I'm here to talk to Mrs. Jennings."

"Might not be the best time at the moment." Squinting, the deputy looked over Glen's shoulder. "Is that Shannon O'Brien? She looks so much like her mama, I'd know her anywhere."

Glen turned to see her nod in the deputy's direction, but she took her sweet time reaching them, first brushing back the stray hairs that had come loose from her braid. This was a small town, so it wouldn't be unusual for the deputy to know residents, but why the undercurrents?

"Hi, Sam. Uh, Deputy Kroeger." Her voice was a bare whisper. She was acting awkward, even a bit intimidated—rare for Shannon.

Kroeger eyed her, and his mouth twisted into a grin. "How're those folks of yours doing? I hear your daddy lost his job. Too bad after all those years of—"

"He's okay." Shannon swallowed. "Mom is great, too."

Frowning, Glen looked at Shannon. She rarely spoke of her parents.

"Nice to hear, darlin'." The deputy nodded. "Hope he's not self-medicating again. Reminds me, I've got to go check up on them sometime soon."

Self-medicating? Glen could only imagine what that meant. A spasm of some unpleasant emotion passed over Shannon's face. Fear? Dread?

Glen held his tongue. An intriguing exchange, to say the least.

A petite woman walked out the front door. "Oh, you must be Shannon. I'm Lucy. I should have called, but I forgot in all the trouble." She frowned at Glen.

Shannon appeared relieved to focus elsewhere. "This is Glen." She pointed at him. "He's the one I told you about.

He owns the shop next to mine." She glanced quickly at the deputy, then straightened her shoulders and looked back at Lucy. "Are you okay?"

"No." Lucy rubbed her arms. "My house has been broken into."

"That's dreadful," Glen said, a feeling of apprehension flooding him. "Is everyone all right?"

"Yes." The woman waved her hand. "And I don't have your box right now. Amber took it with her to her cousin's house last night. They live near us, and the girls go to the same school. They were working on a project together, so I just let her spend the night. I was going to pick her up this afternoon." She clenched her small hands together. "I went grocery shopping this morning, but my house was broken into while I was out. Lucky it wasn't the weekend. Amber wasn't home when that gun-toting killer ransacked our home."

Glen winced. "A gun-toting killer?"

"Now, now," Kroeger said. "We don't have much violent crime in these parts. Mostly minor things. Drinking to excess. Drugs." His gaze fell on Shannon, then back to Glen. "Must've been a teen looking to make a fast buck, then got scared and ran away."

Lucy shuddered. "But nothing was stolen. Not even my new TV. I feel so violated."

Shannon patted Lucy's arm. "I'm sorry. You must be terrified."

Lucy nodded. "Yes. I'm waiting for my husband to come home. I'll have to get back to you about the box, okay? I know you need it. I have your number."

Glen could hear himself trying to explain the delay to Amanda Franklin. "I'd appreciate that." He looked at Kroeger, whose dark, bushy brows were drawn in a frown. "Thank you, Deputy."

Kroeger nodded his way, then smiled at Shannon who whirled around and walked back to the truck with hurried steps. The deputy's radio crackled, and he spoke into it as Glen turned and followed Shannon, questions running through his mind.

How would he explain this to Amanda? And what was the meaning of the odd exchange between Shannon and the deputy?

four

As she mindlessly picked at the strings of her guitar, Shannon looked across her kitchen table at Ray. "I'm glad you came when I invited you for tea. I've had a lousy day. Sheer madness. I want to get it all thought through before I go to Bible study tonight."

Ray wrapped his hands around his mug. "Okay, shoot."

She hugged her guitar closer to her chest. "My past came back to haunt me." *In front of Glen Caldwell of all people.* She recalled seeing Deputy Kroeger, and her peace of mind was severely challenged. She gave Ray a brief rundown about the spice box, then jabbed her index finger on the tabletop. "Do you want to know what that officer of the law did?"

A tiny smile quirked the side of Ray's mouth. "I have a feeling you're going to tell me."

"He said he was going to visit my parents. Yeah, that's what Daddy needs after losing his job and all." She scowled. "My folks don't do the things they used to do. Why'd he imply that? I hate to say this, Ray, because I'm a Christian, but I don't like cops."

"C'mon, Shan. You know they're human like anybody else. You got the good and the bad. And sometimes it's easy to misinterpret their actions and tone." Ray rested his arms loosely on his thighs. "Hey, girl. You're not going to let a visit to Benton City take you to the bad place, are you?"

"It's strange, but living back in this area has diminished my self-confidence. I don't understand it." She set aside her guitar and shrugged. "Glen picked up on Deputy Kroeger's remarks, even though he didn't ask questions on the way home. Glen's as perceptive as they come."

"Well, to change the subject, I think you like this guy," Ray said matter-of-factly. "In fact, I think you more than like him."

"Guy? You mean Glen?" Shannon's heart thumped. "Wow. Is it that obvious to you? If it is, then it must be true, and I haven't really faced it."

"'Fraid so." Ray shrugged.

"Is it my body language?"

He stroked his chin thoughtfully. "It's in your expression plus in your voice when you talk about him."

"Wow. That's scary. I wonder if Glen sees it, too." She looked into Ray's eyes and recalled their conversation a couple of months back. He'd spoken of an ex-fiancée named Bailey. That he'd fallen for her the first time he laid eyes on her until the day he'd caught her dating a guy whom Ray had considered a friend.

"I'm not sure that Glen's on to you, though. Men are dense sometimes. Don't see what's going on right in front of our noses."

"Well, I'm not sure *like* is the right word," Shannon said. "Glen and I always quarrel."

"Whoa." Ray blew out a long whistle. "I hope you like him. It'd be a problem to fall in love with someone you don't like."

"Is that possible?" A spate of nerves weakened her stomach.

"Absolutely it is. It's more like infatuation, I think. You see what you want to see, and in your head they are what you think they are, not what they *really* are."

"Yikes, that sounds like something I'd say." Leaning back in her chair, she considered his weighty comment. "I know I'm idealistic. I'm a lot like my parents that way. I'm scared, Ray. I've never felt this way about any man. I'm not sure what I see in Glen. I'm tofu; he's meat and potatoes."

Ray laughed, crossed his arms, and studied her for a long moment. "Opposites, right? That was me and Bailey. You and I are emotional and driven by our feelings. People like them have a lot of self-discipline and. . ."

And we don't. He didn't have to finish the sentence.

"But what do I know, Shan? Look at me." Ray spread his arms. "I left my career behind. Now I'm going on thirty, doing a gig in a coffeehouse."

Ray never talked about his career, but he'd walked away from whatever work he'd done. Now he lived in a room in someone's basement, played in a band, and gave guitar lessons. How did he survive? He'd said something about taking leave, but never went into detail, and she never asked. Tears stung her eyes. God had put Ray into her life for a reason, and she wanted to encourage him.

"Don't put yourself down, Ray. You're a musical genius." She meant it from the heart. "What I wouldn't give to play like you. You're following your dream is all."

"When do dreams become escape from reality? When does running from reality and following a dream become irresponsibility? And as far as Bailey is concerned? No sense going over that again." Ray jutted his chin to the wall adjoining her apartment with Glen's shop. "Maybe it wouldn't be that way with you and Caldwell—maybe it'll be okay."

Shannon shrugged. "Well, he does make me laugh. He's always giving me advice like he wants me to succeed. He tells me how to keep my books, how to hire employees, and how to clean up my store. I can't figure out if that means he cares or if he's a control freak." She paused and then stared intently at Ray. "You never talk about your past except in snippets."

The words were out before she recognized the deep sadness in Ray's brown eyes. Shannon held up her hand. "I'm sorry. I didn't mean—"

"It's okay. Don't apologize. But the past has no place in the here and now."

"I don't know if I agree with that," Shannon said. "Don't you think the past defines us? At least in part?"

Ray shrugged and stared at the wall. "I'd like to think not. When the Lord comes in, He wipes the past away."

"Yes, but He doesn't erase it. Neither does He change our personalities. What we become is formed by what we've lived, as well as who we are." Shannon picked up her guitar, plucked at a string, and it snapped. "Oh man, I don't have any others."

"I'll bring you a new set tomorrow. I have an appointment in town, anyway."

"Thanks." She leaned her guitar against the table. "I can't tell you how many times I've asked God to give me a personality transplant. So I could be organized and not so weird. And then maybe I would make someone a suitable girlfriend. I have so many doubts about myself lately. Like I'm going through a second adolescence or something."

Ray laughed. "Moving to a new place and everything that's happening here will do that to you." The sadness left his eyes. "Shannon, when you find the right man, he will love you for exactly who and what you are. I've often thought it was too bad you and I don't feel that way about each other."

Shannon grinned. "Yeah, there is that. Venus thought we were dating. But I feel like you're my brother."

"Ouch." Ray mockingly winced and put his fist on his heart. "Handed the brother card."

She laughed. "I guess there has to be some of the opposite traits in a romance. Opposites are drawn to each other, that's for sure. Like my best friend Allie and her husband Derrick. Opposite in many ways, but they're a perfect match."

Ray nodded. "True. It depends on the people involved and whether or not they're willing to accept certain things. Iron sharpens iron." He eyed her from under lowered lids. "So, what about Glen?"

"I don't know." Shannon's gaze scanned her kitchen and the odds and ends piled around that she promised herself she'd get rid of some day. "I'm thinking it would be Oscar Madison and Felix Unger."

Ray laughed. "Yeah, something like that, but I'm beginning to suspect this goes much deeper."

Shannon nodded her heartfelt agreement. "Much."

❧

Dreams of Shannon, her hair shining in shades of gold and her outrageous outfits, filled Glen's mind. Unfortunately they were mixed with thoughts of the difficulties she was causing in his life. All that added to his concern about the missing spice box. The growing list of problems rattled uncontrolled through Glen's brain, keeping him up half the night. He finally fell asleep early Thursday morning, only to wake to the alarm an hour later with a dull, throbbing headache—and the knowledge of what the day would bring. The prospect of facing Amanda Franklin this morning made him want to burrow deeper under the covers. She would be out for blood—Shannon's.

All this trouble, and for what? Because Shannon hadn't heeded his advice. Instead of hiring help based on an outstanding job application and solid references, Shannon used some sort of pity meter with which she favored the likes of Venus. He'd tried to talk to Shannon about the urgency of improving the appearance of her shop on the way home from Lucy Jennings' house, but she interrupted him with chatter about diet and health. He hadn't gotten a chance to ask about her father. She was so frustrating at times, yet he had to admire her ability to accept people and see beyond their outer appearance. She gave people the world saw as losers the benefit of the doubt, a second chance, and wasn't that what the Lord did, too? So what if she sometimes made a bad judgment call? What had Venus really done wrong besides try to imitate Shannon? Yes, it was irresponsible, but she was still a teenager.

Glen sighed. He had no choice but to face the day. He threw back the bedclothes, rolled to the edge of his king-size bed, put his feet to the wood floor, and shivered.

Amanda would continue to make life miserable for Shannon, and as long as she refused to heed his advice, he couldn't defend her the way he wished. And there he was, back to that issue again. Getting Shannon O'Brien to listen to him.

He staggered to the kitchen and put a kettle of water on for tea. While he soft-boiled an egg, he smiled. Fred, the man he'd bought his antique store from, had gotten him hooked on soft-boiled eggs. They'd had many a talk about the antiques over breakfasts. The old family friend, who had moved to Kennewick to be near his mother, had noticed Glen's interest in antiques when he was a teenager. After he moved to the States, he'd kept in contact.

Glen put two slices of bread into the toaster and waited. Once everything was ready, he sat at the table and opened his Bible. "Lord, please speak to me. I need wisdom."

Glen turned to the book of Matthew. A passage in chapter 18, which he'd highlighted in yellow, caught his eye first.

"See that you do not look down on one of these little ones. For I tell you that their angels in heaven always see the face of my Father in heaven. What do you think? If a man owns a hundred sheep, and one of them wanders away, will he not leave the ninety-nine on the hills and go to look for the one that wandered off? And if he finds it, I tell you the truth, he is happier about that one sheep than about the ninety-nine that did not wander off. In the same way your Father in heaven is not willing that any of these little ones should be lost." He reread the passage twice, then again.

A stab of conviction tore through him. In his way, he had been looking down at Shannon, at Venus. Even Ray. He'd held Amanda in a certain odd esteem for far too long, and why? Because she was a major source of his income. Who was the lost sheep in this situation? Himself, or Shannon and her friends?

His cell phone trilled, and Glen scanned the room and discovered it on the kitchen counter. Squinting, he examined the unfamiliar phone number before curiosity got the best of him.

"Glen Caldwell here." There was a long moment of static before he thought he heard his brother's voice. "Thomas, is that you?"

"Glen, I can hear you now. Yes, it's me. I'm calling from a hospital in Haiti."

"What? What's wrong?" The sound of Thomas's voice brought home just how much he missed his younger brother who hadn't had a furlough from the mission field for a long time.

"I can't stay on too long. I'm borrowing a cell phone. But I could use your help."

"Anything, Thomas."

"I know you send us a lot of money monthly, and I hate to ask for more. . .but Melissa. . .the doctor's found a lump. They say it's cancer." Thomas paused with a ragged breath. "We need to get back to London to get her treated properly, and our monthly support doesn't cover these kinds of costs."

Worry knotted Glen's stomach. This was a grim reminder of how badly he needed Amanda's business and why he pandered to her like he did. "How much will you need?"

"Airfare for the six of us. We're taking the kids in case. . .in case we have to stay home for a while. And we need enough to cover a place for us to stay—Mom and Dad don't have room for all of us. And I have to close things down here, pay people to help. I haven't told Dad yet. I'll call him next, but you know his church isn't big. Not a lot of money there."

"Yes, quite true." Glen tried to keep the worry from his voice. Thomas told him how much and where to send the money. "I'll be praying," Glen said when his brother was finished.

"I love you," Thomas said.

"I love you all as well." Glen's throat seized up. "Good-bye for now."

He stood for a long time. Where would he get the money? He'd invested much of his spare cash in large purchases of rare antiques for a job Amanda was doing. She'd given him half as a down payment, but hadn't paid it off yet.

He had no choice but to talk to his friend and banker, Blake. He could add to Glen's revolving line of credit. Reluctantly, Glen dialed the number. After explaining his situation, he snapped his phone closed. Blake had been more than willing. He would do what Glen asked first thing that morning. Of course Blake was willing. The man might be his friend, but he was also a businessman. He would profit from the interest.

He paced. The sooner Amanda paid him, the faster he would be able to restore the money. He opened his phone again and called Amanda, but she didn't answer and he left her a message requesting a meeting that morning.

As he cleaned up his breakfast dishes, the urgency to locate the spice box pressed in on him. Finding the box might mean more time with Shannon, too.

In the bathroom, he grabbed his toothbrush and drew a straight line of paste on the bristles. "Glen, you've never let a woman affect you like this before. Why now? Why Shannon?" He brushed his teeth with a vigor sure to remove enamel. While he swished water in his mouth, he jammed his toothbrush into the holder. Staring into the mirror, he made up his mind. He would try again to reason with Shannon.

❧

Shannon jogged down the stairs from her apartment and stepped into her office. There were a lot of advantages to living where one worked. No commute, for one. But there were also disadvantages. She could never really escape. Truman followed her closely, and she opened the back door to let him outside to do his business.

As she waited, she yawned and rubbed her arms, chilled by the sudden exposure to cold. She hadn't slept well the night before, troubled by thoughts of Amanda, Deputy Kroeger, and, worst of all, Glen and what he must've surmised from the deputy's remarks.

"Come on," she hollered at the dog. She'd pick up his mess in a few minutes. Truman galloped past her and headed for his food bowl. Once inside, Shannon closed her eyes and inhaled deeply of the musty scent of old things mixed with the fragrance of her latest scent passion—cinnamon candles. She opened her eyes again, crossed the room, and glanced into the showroom. Mismatched pieces of furniture were interspersed with shelves of knickknacks, all for sale. The store might look a mess, but she enjoyed repeat business. It felt like home. Her friends loved and accepted her. So why should she care about living up to Glen Caldwell's unrealistic standards? The man was always ready to tell her how to do things better. More efficiently. Glen meant well with his attention to details, but did he really see the big picture? Stop to smell the roses? Was he capable of becoming so absorbed in a project that he engaged the right side of his brain and forgot about the big picture for a little while?

Shannon sighed. She wasn't being fair. Glen wasn't *that* bad. She blew out a breath and withdrew back into her office. Then something caught her eye. On the floor, right beside her desk, lay the purple paper with directions to the Jennings' home. Why hadn't she seen it there yesterday? She thought back to the day before and couldn't remember. Yes, she was messy, but surely she would have noticed. Was stress making her lose her mind? A good possibility, given what she'd studied about the negative effects of stress on the body. She leaned down to pick up the paper when a pounding at her back door made her jump. Truman leaped to life, barked once, and danced around her ankles.

"Who is it?" she yelled, heart pounding.

"Shannon, it's me, Glen."

That figured. Just when she'd been thinking about him. Truman was beside himself, whining with happiness. She shoved him back with her leg and opened the door. Glen's tall form filled the opening. Truman whined louder, and she understood how he felt. Glen looked devastatingly handsome.

"Shannon, you look like you've seen a ghost or something. Can you stop staring and let me in? It's cold."

"Oh, oops. Sorry." She opened the door all the way and stepped aside so he could enter.

Truman greeted him with an enthusiastic bark, and Glen patted the dog's head with a leather-gloved hand.

"What are you doing here?" Shannon asked.

He stepped back and peeled off his gloves, frowning. "What's wrong?"

"You, pounding at the door, scared the wits out of me!" Shannon dangled the paper in front of his eyes. "Look at this. I found it on the floor."

"And?" Glen took another step back. He stared at her as though she'd lost her marbles.

"I know this paper was on the corner of my desk, under the stapler. Then it disappeared, remember? And nobody's been here since our trip to Benton City."

"Yesterday you said it was in your purse."

"That's what I thought, but it wasn't in my purse. You looked. That meant it had to be under the stapler, but it wasn't because I would have seen it. It was on the floor. But I didn't notice it there last night, either."

Glen glanced pointedly around her office. "How would you know?"

Shannon slapped the paper on the desk. "Because I would. It was important."

"All right." Glen held up his hands in a gesture of surrender. "Maybe Venus moved it. And wasn't Ray here?"

Judging by the scowl on his face, Glen had added Ray Reed to his riffraff list. "This paper wasn't here when Venus left last night. And yes, Ray was here." She frowned at him. "Are you spying on me?"

Glen cocked one brow and straightened his already perfect

posture. "Spying? Not likely. But who can miss his comings and goings? The sound of his bike echoes off the buildings in the alley like thunder." He looked her in the eye, sending warmth through her that chased away the chill of the morning. "Perhaps this is a mystery that won't be solved at the moment. In fact, there are more pressing matters at hand. The purple paper aside, we need to have a talk, Shannon."

Why did he have to go and speak her name that way? So warm and inviting. She averted her gaze to the window and the alley behind the stores. "What would you like to talk about?"

"Have you heard from Lucy Jennings?"

"No, not yet." Through the window, Shannon saw a shiny, expensive-looking vehicle pull into the parking lot beyond the alley. It came to a stop, the door opened, and out came Amanda.

"Uh-oh." Shannon swallowed. Amanda marched a straight path to the back door of The Quaint Shop, a fur coat swirling around her leather boots. Shannon's heart banged against her ribs. All she wanted was to remain centered, and here she was filled with dread and a weird jealousy. Amanda was rich and beautiful, with legs to die for—and it was obvious she was attracted to Glen. Shannon read it time and again in Amanda's body language.

"What is it?" Glen asked, coming to stand beside her, so close the scent of his soap made her want to snuggle against him. "Oh great! Amanda. She wasn't due to meet me"—he pulled back his coat sleeve and glanced at his watch—"for another hour, at least."

Shannon had a sudden desperate thought. "I'm going to invite her in for tea and try to reason with her." She reached for the knob on the back door.

"Are you serious?" Glen placed his hand over hers on the knob. "Let me, um, let me take care of this." With his gaze on the fast-approaching Amanda, he said, "You can't handle her."

Shannon jerked her hand from under his, stepped back, and tilted her chin. "Thus far you've done a bang-up job of handling her yourself. Just look at her. Even someone who doesn't know how to read body language could read hers."

Glen nodded. "Yes, well, to use one of your colloquialisms, she looks like she's about to spit nails, but. . ."

Both of them inhaled when Amanda sidestepped the solid door, cupped her hands around her eyes, and glared at them through the windowpane. Why should she bother to knock when she could try to intimidate them through the window with a slit-eyed glare?

Shannon lifted her hand to wave, but Glen grabbed her arm before she could do it.

She tried to shake him off, but he didn't let go. "Stop it, Glen. I was going to do a beauty-queen wave. That hair of hers reminds me—"

"No need to make things worse. Go ahead and open the door," Glen instructed through a tight-lipped smile.

"Oh, now I'm making it worse?" She yanked her arm away from him and glared. "First you say don't open the door, then you say open the door. And they say *women* can't make up their minds." Shannon twisted the doorknob.

five

Glen opened his mouth to remind Shannon that her lack of discretion in hiring quality personnel had caused this problem, but he didn't have time before Amanda pushed her way inside.

"Good morning, Amanda. Come on in," Shannon said in a cordial greeting that only Glen noticed was sarcastic.

"I almost stepped in a pile that dog of yours left." Amanda tried to shove past Shannon, but she stood firm even though her face reddened.

"I'm sorry. Truman was just out, and I haven't had time—"

"Never mind. I wouldn't expect anything else." Amanda stepped around Shannon and directed her gaze straight up into Glen's eyes. "Well, where is it?" She was trembling as she removed her gloves.

"I've already explained to you where it is. Didn't you get my phone message?" He said nothing else as he waited for his anger to subside. Amanda had a colossal nerve dismissing Shannon as if she wasn't there. Shannon's eyes glittered, but Glen had a feeling it was anger more than hurt.

Amanda patted her billowy mane of curls, then laid her fingertips on his arm. Glen resisted the temptation to pull away from her touch.

"You said you were going to get it yesterday; then you call me and tell me you didn't. You said the woman who bought *my* property let her daughter run off with it like it was some sort of insignificant plaything. This is ridiculous." Her hand was shaking despite her bold tone of voice.

"Well, Lucy didn't know any better." Shannon's voice was low but firm, and now Amanda did turn to look at her.

55

"Lucy? Who is Lucy? Your incompetent help?"

Shannon's lips thinned, and Glen knew she was biting her tongue. She'd be proud that he was reading her body language. The cloud of hostility in the office, coupled with the thick scent of Amanda's musky perfume, increased the intensity of his pounding headache, but he kept his face placid.

"Lucy is the woman who bought the box. We're waiting to hear back from her after her daughter returns." Glen cut a glance at Shannon. "Did you get a call from her yet?"

"A call?" Amanda's high-pitched voice pierced his ears. "I won't wait for a call. I'm going to pick up the box myself, which is what I should've done to begin with." She stood between him and Shannon and gave them both a look of disgust. "Now then." She lifted her hand, palm up. "I want that address."

"No. She was my customer. I'll deal with her." Shannon tilted her chin defiantly. Glen was simultaneously irate at Amanda and proud of Shannon. He saw her surreptitiously slip the purple paper into the pocket of her floral skirt. "As soon as Lucy phones, I'll go out to her house to get the spice box."

Amanda's eyes flashed, and her face colored. "Glen? I'd like to have a word with you. . .outside."

"Yes, yes of course."

Shannon began humming. Something familiar. Glen concentrated and then almost choked. It was the song "Cruella de Vil" from *101 Dalmatians*.

Glen took Amanda's arm and hurried her out the back door. Then he glanced over his shoulder at Shannon. Arms crossed, she tossed him an impish grin and shut the door. Hard.

He fumbled with his keys, opened the back door to his store, and held it for Amanda. She brushed past him, then dropped to the edge of his desk. "I didn't want it to come to this," she said through tight lips, "but I've got a thirty-six-thousand-dollar order pending with you."

Glen heard the threat before she spoke it. "The furniture for the Johnson project is nearly complete. We searched high and low for the breakfront you requested." He pushed a smile to his face. "We'll add that piece, and the shipment will arrive tomorrow."

Shaking her head, Amanda slid away from his desk and stood face-to-face with him. "I want that address, Glen, or I'm cancelling the Johnson order."

Her eyes were flashing, and he wondered why the spice box was so important. Its monetary value didn't warrant her behavior. She was known for her fiery temper, but this conduct was over-the-top even for her.

He couldn't afford to lose this order. He couldn't afford to eat the cost. And now his brother needed help desperately. He had no choice but to try to make amends with the unreasonable woman. He was tempted to follow Shannon's example and hum the Disney movie tune.

"I cannot divulge the name of the person who bought the box, but please, will you give me until Monday to get it back to you?"

Seconds ticked by like long minutes while she paced his office, her heels clicking against the tile. Her eyes finally snapped up to his face. "For old time's sake, I'll do it."

His shoulders sagged with relief. "Thank you, Amanda, you won't be sorry."

"Of course I won't be. I hope you won't be." She hoisted her purse strap higher on her shoulder and smiled. "I hope you and I can continue to work together in harmony." Her smile dissolved. "But we have one big thing between us that I want to take care of. Shannon O'Brien. I'm going to see Mike Carroll with the petition."

"What does that mean? How will the petition take care of Shannon?" What kind of hold did she have over Mike to give her such clout?

"You yourself have expressed a desire to have our stores

tidy. You expressed interest in the Renew Our Storefronts project. . .and might I add, you signed the petition."

"Yes, but not at the expense of closing down businesses. I would like to see that petition again."

"I don't have it with me." Shaking her head, Amanda's eyes narrowed, and Glen felt nailed to the wall.

"What?" Glen shrugged. "What is it?"

"I've suspected this for quite some time. Now I know for a certainty." Amanda clucked her tongue. "Shame on you, Glen. Shannon is not your type. Of course you're probably using her. I will need to teach you to have better taste." Her gaze raked him head to toe. "She looks like a peasant from—"

"That's quite enough. You know nothing about Shannon." Amanda had just crossed a line. Client or not, she had no right to speak to him like that about his personal life.

Amanda paled, eyes flashing with anger—Shannon wouldn't have to interpret this body language for him. But he couldn't bring himself to apologize. Instead he walked to the door, grabbed the handle with a tight grip, and pulled it open for her. An icy blast of winter air whirled around him, a perfect accompaniment for Amanda's words and attitude. She'd make him regret what he said. A woman scorned was dangerous, and he'd chosen Shannon over her. Asking for her mercy on Shannon would only strengthen her resolve to get revenge.

He heard the roar of an approaching motorcycle and over Amanda's shoulder saw Ray Reed pull up. Perfect timing. Glen's jaw clenched.

"I am not a small-minded woman," Amanda said.

Glen choked back a rude laugh. The engine noise stopped.

Amanda's brittle smile did not reach her eyes. "I will still allow you until Monday to find the box. And I hope within that time frame you will give thought to the situation at hand." She turned and swept majestically through the opening.

The *situation at hand.* Glen snapped the door closed behind his client.

He could warn Shannon or. . . He paced his office and debated with himself. The sound of raised voices sent him running to the window to look outside. Amanda was in a shouting match with Reed, who looked worse than usual in old, worn jeans and beard stubble on his face. Shannon stood against her door, her big dog at attention beside her. Her eyes looked impossibly large as she watched Amanda and Ray argue. Someone had to do damage control, and she obviously wasn't up to the job. He snatched his coat from the tree stand.

❧

Hand clenched tight around Truman's leash, Shannon could do nothing but watch in silence at the ugly scene before her. She loathed angry confrontation of any kind and wanted only to make peace with Amanda, but the goal somehow eluded her grasp.

"You can't talk to Shannon like she's garbage." Ray slammed his helmet against the seat of his Harley.

Amanda clenched her fists. "No one speaks to me in that tone of voice."

The two glared at each other when the back door to Glen's shop swung open, and he stepped out and walked over to stand next to Shannon.

Amanda sent a scathing glance to Glen, then back to Ray, who was leaning against his bike, arms crossed, staring at Amanda. Truman growled low in his chest.

"Ray was just standing here," Shannon explained in a hurried whisper to Glen, whose face was a mask of controlled anger. "Amanda began yelling at me, and he defended me."

Amanda fisted her hands and jammed them on her hips. "Glen, what are you going to do about this—this riffraff?"

Shannon's heart sank.

"Pardon me," Glen said. "What—"

"He insulted me." Amanda leaned forward, eyes narrowed, savoring the exchange.

Truman stood and pulled at the leash. "That's not true."

Shannon wrapped the leash tighter around her fisted hand. "I saw the whole thing. Please, calm down. You're upsetting my dog." She'd never before heard Truman's menacing growl or seen the fur on his back raised. A sense of dread washed over her.

"Are you calling me a liar?" Amanda stomped her high-heeled boot on the sidewalk. "Glen? Are you listening to me? I may call the police."

Ray snorted rudely. Glen faced him and seemed oblivious to Amanda's query. Neither man backed down.

"Please, Ray, drop it," Shannon said.

Her plea snapped him back to reality, and he raised both his hands as if in surrender. "I don't want any trouble, Caldwell."

"I don't intend to give you any." Glen's promise and his mild tone of voice didn't match his challenging stance. For once, Shannon was stumped by his body language. He glanced over at her, then back at Ray. "But perhaps you could, er, apologize to Amanda for your rudeness."

"Rudeness?" Something unspoken flew between the men; then Ray seemed to reach a conclusion. "Sure. Why not?" He turned toward Amanda, who wore an arrogant grin. "Sorry, ma'am, for any inconvenience." His cold smile was unlike anything Shannon had seen from him before. His gaze snapped to her, and he motioned with his head. "Come on. Let's go inside. I'm ready for some pleasant company."

As Shannon turned to enter her store, the last thing she heard was Amanda Franklin say to Glen, "Now do you see what I mean?"

≈

Glen trailed Amanda to her car and braced himself for her wrath. Amanda would expect him to take sides, a lose-lose proposition in this situation. How could he protect Shannon—and his business—and not lose the money he so desperately needed to keep his commitment to his brother?

"Amanda," Glen said to her back when she stopped next

to her car. He sent up a silent prayer for conciliatory words. "Remember what I said? If for whatever reason the spice box is gone, I will pay you for what it's worth. Then I will help you find another just like it. Please understand that."

"And remember that I said it's insured," she snapped. "The money is not the point. I want *that* box."

"I'm sorry. I'm doing everything I can. Shannon's clerk, Venus, didn't sell your spice box with ill intent. Your mom—"

"You're allowing your feelings for Shannon to take precedence over the safety concerns of your neighbors and faithful clients." Amanda didn't face him.

Whatever that had to do with the box. "I don't know what 'feelings' we're discussing here, but I've always addressed every one of your concerns." *The whole stinking lot of complaints*, he was tempted to add.

She whirled around. "Your love life is of no consequence to me, not unless it interferes with business. Shannon O'Brien's been nothing but trouble since the day she parked that filthy truck full of broken furniture on our street."

Her anger-laced words said more than anything else that his "love life" was indeed of consequence to her. And suddenly the root of her anger at Shannon became clear. She was jealous.

Amanda crossed her arms over her midsection and blew out a breath. "And worse, people are afraid to shop here. Look at the type of element she brings around."

Glen couldn't agree that things were that bad. Still, if Shannon had cooperated with him, he could counter Amanda's claims, but he found himself at a loss.

"You've got until Monday to get me that box. Then I will present Mike with the petition and proceed with a lawsuit, and you will never work for me again." She spun around, opened her car door, and got inside. Without another glance at him, she started the engine and drove away. Gritting his teeth, he headed back to his shop.

Ray Reed had defended Shannon against Amanda, and Glen had tried to defend her in his own way but couldn't to the extent he wished without alienating his client.

On a sigh, Glen went back inside his office and sat at his desk. Amanda might be jealous, but that had little to do with her desire to get back the box. Something wasn't adding up here.

His thoughts were interrupted by the dim sound of voices and off-key plunks on guitar strings coming through the wall from next door. A sudden burst of jealousy pumped lava through his veins. Glen stood and jammed his hands in his pockets.

Despite late-night arguments with himself about Shannon, he was losing the battle with the logical part of his mind. His feelings for her had been growing for a long time, but he'd kept himself busy, avoided being with her, and compartmentalized his emotions. He kept reminding himself that he needed a mate who was orderly and rational, not a goofy flower child who wanted to befriend the world and didn't seem to have an organized bone in her body.

Glen returned to his seat and flipped open a folder on his desk. Time to get to work. He had to get Shannon off his mind and concentrate on business. His dad told him to trust God with every problem. Until Shannon O'Brien barged into his life and rattled his cage, he thought he had a handle on "let go and let God," but she forced him to take the reins again. "God, please help me put all of this in Your hands."

Tomorrow he'd meet with Mike Carroll. Find out how badly Amanda had already poisoned Mike's mind against Shannon and convince him that she wasn't a lost cause. Then he'd help Shannon fix up her store. . .if she'd allow him.

six

"There you go." Ray handed Shannon the guitar from where he sat in the leather chair. "The new string is on, but you'll have to keep tuning it for a few days. New strings don't hold their tune well."

"Okay, thanks." She took the guitar, strummed a few chords, then started to cry.

"Hey," he said softly and patted her arm. "Don't let that skinny hag disturb your balance."

Shannon giggled through her tears, almost choking herself. "That's not nice, Ray. Well, she's skinny, but she's not a hag. She's beautiful."

He rolled his eyes. "That's a matter of opinion. Or should I say, *taste*. But she's definitely not nice. Beauty is what beauty does, you know. And she's got it in for you."

Placing her guitar on her desk, Shannon sniffled, then swiped her arm over her face. "I do pray for her, and I ask God to forgive me for my awful thoughts. I just don't understand. I haven't done anything bad to her. Well, I guess I have. Amanda almost stepped in a pile of Truman's poop. I forgot to clean it up." She sighed. "What's wrong with me?"

"You have faults like everyone else," he said. "It's just that yours are manifested on the outside. Some people seem perfect because their faults are more internal."

"That sounds weirdly like something I would say." Shannon frowned. "Is that why Amanda doesn't like me? That's why she's upset? Because I'm a slob?"

He grinned. "You really don't know why she's upset?"

"I figured it was my shop. I'm a blight to the other store owners."

"That might be part of it, but it's not all." Ray grabbed her guitar and expertly picked at the strings.

"Okay, I'll bite. Why does she hate me?"

Ray's grin widened, and then he laughed. "That's one of the things I find so refreshing about you. Your total naivety."

Shannon frowned while she watched his fingers pluck the strings. "I don't think I'm naive at all. You know about my past. How my dad got busted for drugs. They did it around me. I—"

"You are still amazingly innocent despite your past." Ray stopped playing the guitar. "Your parents weren't the hardened criminal types. I'm not saying what they did was right—it wasn't. They were just free spirits who lived the way they wanted. Unfortunately, illegal activity is illegal activity, and you saw the results."

"That aside, why does Amanda hate me?"

"Because Glen more than likes you."

"What? You think so?"

"I made a special effort to watch him today." He put the guitar down and zipped his leather jacket. "I gotta get going, but trust me on this, Shannon."

☙

That afternoon Shannon ran from her office, waving a piece of paper and punching the air, yelling, "Thank You, Lord!" She'd been waiting all day for Lucy's call, and finally it had come.

Venus was staring at shards of ceramic on the floor. "I'm sorry. I broke a vase. It's kind of crowded in here." The teen glanced at Shannon with wide eyes rimmed on the bottom with dark half-moons.

"So I've heard. It's okay. Just sweep it up." Shannon tripped over an unopened box in her way and dropped the paper. It landed near the pieces of vase, and Venus picked it up. "What's this?"

"The address where the box is. Lucy called. Her daughter

left it there. Mystery solved." Shannon paused. "You know, the whole thing is really weird. The person who broke into the Jennings' house didn't take anything. It makes me wonder. . . . Anyway, the Allman family is expecting me tomorrow morning."

"Good, Shan. That's great."

"Are you okay? You look tired."

"I'm fine." Venus handed Shannon the directions, took a broom from behind the counter, and began to sweep with lethargic movements. Her cell phone began playing a popular tune, and she jumped.

"Yes, I think it's great, too." Shannon put the paper with the Allmans' address next to the cash register. "Go on and get your phone. I'm going next door. I'll be right back."

Shannon exited her store, circumvented the stacked furniture outside her shop, and turned into Glen's doorway.

"Shannon, um, Ms. O'Brien," Charlie said with a warm smile. "Can I help you?"

"Call me Shannon, please. Is Glen here?"

"Yes, I am." Glen appeared from the back of the store and strode toward her. Ray's words came back to her, and she felt suddenly shy and awkward. Her gaze scattered, first on Glen's broad shoulders, then his hair, and finally his face.

Big mistake. His crystal blue eyes held her gaze. Charlie said something, but she was focused on trying to interpret the meaning behind Glen's expression. Was Ray right?

"I, um. . ." Shannon pointed in the general direction of her store. "Got a call from Lucy."

Glen slipped his hands into his pockets and leaned against the counter.

Charlie cleared his throat. "Did they find where the box went?"

Glen continued to look at her in an odd, assessing way. She didn't know whether to be worried or elated, but she was leaning toward worried.

"Yes." Shannon glanced at Charlie, then swallowed and started again. "Lucy's daughter left the box at her friend's house in her upset state over the break-in." She dug in her coat pocket. "Oh, I must've left the address in my store." She brushed her hand over her long braid. Why was Glen staring? "Anyway, the place is only a couple miles from Lucy's house." She took two steps backward toward the door. Glen pushed off the dresser and walked toward her. "And—and I'll leave first thing tomorrow morning to get it. Everything will turn out fine after all."

"I'm going with you, of course."

Wagging her head, her pulse soared. Her emotions were making it impossible to read Glen's body language. He leaned toward her with a trace of a smile on his handsome face. Was Ray right?

"You won't want to join me, Glen. Remember last time?"

"Mr. Caldwell." Charlie cleared his throat. "May I go next door for a minute?"

"Yes," Glen said, but kept his gaze on her.

Shannon heard the chimes, felt the cold draft sweep in from the door as Charlie walked out.

"I suspect Charlie's taken with Venus."

"Do you?" *And are you taken with me?* she wanted to ask. *Do you want to hold me in your arms?* "What makes you say that?"

Glen took a step closer. "Body language."

Shannon giggled nervously. "What do you know about body language, Glen Caldwell?"

He looked directly into her eyes again, and her heart pounded madly. "I might know a bit more than you suspect, Shannon O'Brien."

Did he mean he could see through to her heart? Her face heated. "So then, I've got to get going. I'll have the box back to you by tomorrow afternoon."

"I am going with you."

"No way!" She couldn't be in a closed vehicle with him

again. She was afraid her feelings for him had grown to the point that she wouldn't be able to conceal them. "I'm taking Truman with me. You know what happened last time."

"You know, Truman's starting to grow on me." Glen's little smile made her heart pound faster. He was so close she could reach up and. . .

"What time will you be leaving, Shannon?"

Why'd he have to go and speak her name again in that subtle tone of his? "What time?" Yikes, she sounded like a parrot. "You're not a morning person, Glen. I'm leaving very early."

He chuckled at her reminder. "Tomorrow will be nothing like our first trip." His eyes held a mischievous twinkle. "I think I'm prepared this time."

His gaze traveled over her face. He might be prepared, but she wasn't—not at all. She tried to regain her balance, but it had totally left her. *Lord*. . . "It's up to you. I'm leaving at seven thirty so I can be back to open my shop on time."

"I'll be there."

Shannon pivoted and ducked out of his shop before she had a chance to open her mouth again. "Okay," she whispered and began to pray. As she walked into her shop, she settled in her mind that she'd fallen in love with Glen. In His time, the Lord would iron out the wrinkles in their relationship—or not.

seven

On Friday morning as Shannon's truck jounced over the interstate and Truman lapped his ear, Glen settled back stoically. He had no choice but to accompany her on the early morning trip. He needed to hold the elusive spice box in his hands and then give it to Amanda on a silver platter if necessary.

Anger heated his face. What could be worse than to be beholden to Amanda—to be unable to defend Shannon publicly just to keep Amanda happy? Today his mission was twofold: Get the box and hope that would quell her antagonism toward Shannon so Amanda wouldn't pressure Mike Carroll to kick Shannon out—and at the same time hold on to Amanda's brisk business in order to pay off his debt.

"Want tea?" Shannon reached around Truman and handed him a thermos.

He gave her an appreciative nod and met her gaze for a moment. "Thank you." Who was he kidding? His mission was threefold. While listening to Shannon and Ray practice guitar through the thin wall that separated their shops, it hit him how deeply he'd grown to care for her during the past year, and much more during the past few days. He wanted the disorganized shopgirl to stay in her store. To stay in his life. Perhaps nothing would come of their association, but he was willing to try.

"You're awfully quiet." Shannon shot him a curious look. "I'm worried. You haven't even complained about Truman yet."

Glen concealed his smile under a frown. "I was just about to lodge a complaint, but after yesterday's display of Truman's temper, I figured it was best not to get on his bad side."

"I'm sorry about that. It was unexpected."

"Amanda was hostile, and it was directed toward you. I can't fault Truman for his actions."

Truman flopped his immense head against Glen's shoulder at the mention of his name, panting warm moisture on his face.

"Truman, back off," Shannon ordered in a soft tone. Wolf-dog obeyed immediately. "I wonder if I've got better animal skills than people skills. You think?"

"I think your people skills are fine. You care deeply, and people know that. . ."

"But," she said. "I can hear the 'but' at the end of that sentence."

"You don't always use wisdom." In fact, her life could be much easier if she'd allow him to help. How could he get through to her? "You've collected a few foes along the way. People who don't understand you. It happens to everyone."

"I know I'm different." She shifted in the seat and swiped a stray hair from her face. "It was always that way," she added softly.

"Truly?" Glen took another sip of the delicious tea, staring, waiting with interest for a deeper revelation. The rusted truck idled loudly at the STOP sign, and Shannon looked at him with her quizzical hazel eyes as if to see if he were serious or perhaps if he could be trusted.

"What I meant to say was. . ." What exactly did he mean to say? Searching the depths of her eyes, he'd be sure to slip out with something he'd later regret. "You're charming, is all. And some people just don't see it."

Shannon's face colored, and she quickly looked away from him.

"I meant that as a compliment, of course." Glen adjusted his glasses and studied her. There seemed to be a hiccup in their communication—an unbreachable chasm that prevented them from fully understanding one another.

"Thank you," Shannon said belatedly. "Um, Bible study this week at church was about sowing and reaping—"

"Ah yes. A good topic to study," Glen said. A discussion on scripture should be safer terrain.

"You know what I don't get? I'm trying to sow good things with Amanda, but it's not working." A small line formed between her brows, and he resisted the urge to lean over and press a kiss to her full lips.

"Out of control," he whispered.

Her head jerked toward him. "Huh?"

Wait. That's how he felt about her. "That is, er, some situations are out of our control. Amanda overreacted. Unfortunately, I depend on her business."

Shannon's frown deepened. "You *need* Amanda's business?" She slowed the truck to a crawl. "I guess I imagined from the looks of your store that you were wealthy."

He laughed. "Don't I wish. Despite appearances, I don't have oodles of cash, and Amanda's purchases bring in a good portion of my earnings."

&

Shannon's heart sank. "You're scaring me, Glen. I feel like crying for the trouble I've caused you." She took the exit to Benton City with greater urgency. "Don't worry, we'll get the spice box and make Amanda happy—whatever 'happy' means to Amanda Franklin."

His lips turned up in a half smile, bringing her a measure of relief. She didn't have Glen figured out. She had put him in a box—confident, organized, and bossy, not to mention wealthy. Believing those things had made her feel he deserved her jabs. She, who prided herself in reading body language and understanding people. She'd failed with Glen. Perhaps her acceptance of people was reserved only for those who needed her. Those who didn't, she either avoided or believed they were too good for her. She rubbed her forehead with her left hand. It was all too complicated, and thinking about it made her head throb.

"I've said it before, but I'm sorry, Glen."

"No need to apologize. I can come off as overbearing, even when I'm just trying to help. I've got to work on that." Glen patted Truman's head. "But I do need Amanda's business. My brother is a missionary, and his wife is ill. She has to travel back to London from Haiti to get the treatment she needs, and they don't have the money."

"Can't their home church help? And don't they have monthly support like most missionaries? What about the organization they work under?"

Glen's sad smile didn't reach his eyes. "Their home church is my dad's church, as well as the organization they work under. My father is the pastor. But it's small, and right now things aren't great financially for the congregation. Yes, they have monthly support, but it won't cover these expenses. I borrowed money to wire to Thomas. I didn't really have it to give."

"Wow, your father and brother are in the ministry?" Shannon felt a sinking sensation in her stomach.

"Yes. I wasn't called to the ministry, but I work to support both of them as I can. If I lose Amanda's business—"

"You won't. I promise." Shannon scanned the directions to the Allman house. This time she had taped the paper to her dashboard. "We'll be there in five minutes. We'll get the spice box and give it to Amanda."

"All's well that ends well."

Would this end well? Maybe for Glen, his family, and Amanda, but a romance between her and Glen? The divide had just grown deeper. He might not be the blue blood she'd imagined, but now it was worse. Introducing a man from a good religious family to her parents. No, she could never do that.

"So where's your father's church?"

"Back in London."

Time for a change of topic lest their chat turn to questions about her family background. Lois and John O'Brien were still in their broken-down trailer. They had always meant to do better—just as she always meant to get her act together. Finish projects she'd started, just like her father and mother whose yard, trailer, and outbuildings were stuffed with things they'd never completed. A loom and spinning wheel from the time her mother raised sheep in order to spin wool. And the table her father built for a train set he'd never bought. She forced her mind back to Glen. "So what church do you attend?"

"Tri-Cities Tabernacle," Glen said. "How about you?"

"I'm at Sanctuary of Praise."

"Ah, Pastor Zach's church. I know him. That was the first church I attended when I moved from London to the Tri-Cities."

Shannon's throat grew tight. Pastor Zach and his wife Laurie would never reveal anything she had confided in them. Still, the idea that Glen knew her minister made her want to run away and reinvent herself all over again. "Why do you attend Tri-Cities Tabernacle if you've got a friendship with Pastor Zach?"

A long silence hung between them, and she told herself not to jump to an ugly conclusion. The people in Glen's church were wealthy. She'd hate to think he'd made his choice based on the opportunity to network.

"I guess I began attending there because many of my clients did." He took a deep breath. "That doesn't sound great, does it?"

She said nothing. Glen put a high priority on business, but in a different way than she did. She also cared just as much for people, and that was often her downfall. Maybe men in general prioritized differently than women.

"Come to think of it, I think I'll attend your church this Sunday. Say hello to Zach and Laurie."

Shannon wanted to scream "no". She was scheduled to give her testimony in front of the congregation this Sunday.

She'd shrivel in embarrassment if Glen was there listening. "Maybe you should try for Sunday after next. We're having a Thanksgiving service and fellowship afterward. I think you'll enjoy it more."

Glen leaned forward in the seat. "Look at that. Either we have a deputy escort waiting for us or there's trouble up ahead."

"What?" Shannon squinted, and her eyes lit on the flashing lights up ahead. "Oh no. Don't tell me that's the Allman house."

They got closer, and one of her least favorite people was there. Deputy Kroeger stood with his hands fisted on his hips. When she pulled in front of the house, he pointed to a spot behind his car. She parked and turned off the engine to the tune of her pulse roaring in her ears.

&

Glen tightened his hands into fists. Was this to be a repeat of last time? If he couldn't get the spice box, Amanda would make good on her threat to take business away from him. And there would be no way to talk her out of trying to get Shannon evicted.

Glen exited the truck and Shannon jumped from her side with her purse over her shoulder, leaving Truman inside.

Deputy Kroeger approached them with long strides. Glen felt Shannon shrinking against him, and he enjoyed the sensation, even while he wondered at her reaction. He put an arm around her shoulder, and she allowed him to leave it there.

"What do you folks want?" the deputy asked. He turned his full attention on Shannon. "You know anything about this?"

"About what? What's happened?" Shannon jabbed her elbow into Glen's side. Did she mean for him to speak up on her behalf?

"We're here to buy back the same antique from the Allmans that we wanted from Lucy Jennings. Her daughter left it here."

Glen eyed the rundown house. "Is there a problem?"

"So, they were expecting you?" Kroeger nodded slowly, like he was onto something big.

"Yes," Glen said. "What's going on?"

"Another break-in." Kroeger tilted his head. "What are the odds? I'm wondering. What's the deal with this box? Tell me what you know about it."

That was a good question. Glen was beginning to think the "deal" with the box was much more than what appeared on the surface. "It's a valuable antique that was sold accidentally. The original owner wants it back."

Shannon pulled away from him, and he let his arm drop. "Where is the family?" she asked. "Are they okay?"

"George took his wife and daughters to his parents' house. I'm waiting for him to come back. I guess they forgot about you in the trauma of having their house broken into."

Glen nodded, feeling selfish. He hadn't even considered the family's feelings.

"So this box is valuable, you say?" Kroeger's expression had changed. His eyes lost their focus, and a deep groove appeared between his eyebrows.

"Yes, a bit," Glen said. "Surely you can imagine why the owner is eager to have it returned."

Kroeger's attention snapped back to Glen. He removed a notebook from his pocket, along with a pen. "Who owns this box?"

Glen exchanged a glance with Shannon. Looking vulnerable, she shrugged and waited for him to talk. "The owner is a woman named Amanda Franklin."

The deputy met Glen's gaze. "Franklin, you say? You mean the James Franklin family in Kennewick?"

"Yes." Glen prayed Kroeger wouldn't hassle Amanda. That was all he needed.

"I see." Kroeger scribbled something in the notebook, then slapped it shut. "I need numbers where I can reach both of you."

Glen pulled a leather business card holder from his shirt pocket. Shannon began digging into her purse. "Do you know if the spice box was stolen?" She glanced up at the deputy.

"Don't know." Kroeger eyed both of them in turn.

Shannon finally found a business card. Glen eyed the crinkled card with dog-eared corners.

"If you folks don't mind now, I have a job to do. I might even call you and tell you if the box is here. And Shannon, tell your daddy I said hello." He turned and with his slow, sure gait walked back to his vehicle.

&

Shannon realized her fingers were going numb and released her death grip on the steering wheel. *Stop it!* She was a new creation in Christ. She wasn't the six-year-old girl, shaking and wrapped in a blanket on her bed as deputies rummaged through her parents' trailer in search of their stash while they were handcuffed in the living room. She especially remembered the young Deputy Kroeger, standing in the doorway to her bedroom, staring at her with a blank expression before going back to scream at her parents and arrest her father.

Glen cleared his throat. "Shannon?"

Now what? She wished Glen hadn't come along. Not only had they run into the deputy again, she'd made a fool of herself, pressing up against Glen like a lovesick teenager. But she had to admit that his strong arm felt so good around her shoulders.

Leave the past in the past, she ordered herself. Too many things were pressing in the present to dwell there. "Two burglaries, Glen. Kroeger's right. What are the chances?"

"Right." Glen shoved Truman's head away as the dog made several attempts to lick his face.

"What's with that box? It's like a trouble magnet." Shannon drew deep breaths. "You don't think it's possible that Amanda..." She let her words drift away.

Glen's gaze snapped toward her. "You mean you wonder if

Amanda is behind the break-ins?"

"That's horrible of me, isn't it? Especially since we don't even know if the box is missing yet." Shannon shook her head. "I can't believe I'd think something so ugly." She understood Glen's long silence to mean he was furious with her. "I'm sorry."

"Don't be. The thought crossed my mind as well. I just don't know how she'd know who had the box."

"What will we do if it's gone?"

Glen shrugged. Shannon fought rising fear that raised goose bumps on her arms. "I'm sure Amanda will go into cardiac arrest if we can't find it." Biting hard on her lower lip, she vowed to stay away from her old stomping grounds. The memories brought on by the close proximity dredged up old fears and brought out the worst in her. She totally lost her balance and any confidence she had worked hard to develop. She took a deep, cleansing breath and asked the Lord for peace. After a minute she slapped her hand on the steering wheel.

"If the box is gone, I'll find it if it's the last thing I do, pay whatever it costs to get it back, and put an end to all this craziness. Although I don't know how."

"It's obvious that box is worth more than Amanda is letting on." Glen clutched the dashboard in a white-knuckle grip. "Please slow down."

Shannon lifted her foot off the gas pedal. "Sorry, I didn't realize I was speeding." The truck slowed, and Glen sat back again. "Will you tell Amanda about this? About the break-in?"

Glen snorted. "As you Americans say, 'No way, Jose.' I'll put it off as long as possible and hope the box is sitting in the Allmans' house. Amanda gave me until Monday to find the box or—"

"Or what?" Shannon's heart filled with dread.

"She'll take her business away from me."

Shannon's stomach turned over, and she thought she might have to stop the truck so she could be sick on the roadside. "Amanda said that?"

"Yes." Glen glanced at her around Truman. "I have to trust the Lord is in control. There's no point in getting uptight."

"Uptight? Uptight?" Fear and anger made her voice high-pitched and loud. Anger at Amanda for her controlling ways. Fear that she'd take business from Glen. Anger at Deputy Kroeger for reminding her of the past. Fear that Glen would find out just what her childhood was like. Anger at her parents for being weird. And even anger at Glen for talking to her in hippie-speak. She'd heard that expression enough times from her parents to make her stomach twist in knots. "I'm not *uptight*. I think everything is just *groovy*."

"Groovy?" Glen raked his fingers through his hair, then stared out the passenger-side window.

She'd done it again—managed to scare off another normal guy. And this time she had unleashed anger on top of it. Try as she might to reinvent the Shannon who reflected the image of her parents, Benton City brought it back home to her. Now things were worse. She was developing a temper. She shook her head. Of all people to see that, why the handsome, charming Glen Caldwell?

She glanced around Truman at Glen and saw his shoulders shaking. "Are you crying?" she asked in disbelief.

Glen shifted his gaze to her again, and she saw the grin on his face. "No. Have you cooled down a bit?"

"You're laughing?"

"Yes."

"There is nothing to laugh about here. Stop it."

"Oh, but there is," he said. "It's a comedy of errors. Us chasing a box all over the place." Truman stuck his nose in Glen's ear, and he shoved it away. "So why are you irritable? It's not like you."

"Oh, let me see," Shannon said. "We both might be sued. Amanda hates my guts. The box is missing, and Kroeger looked at me cross-eyed."

The dog rested his head on Glen's shoulder. "Cross-eyed?

Is that another one of your American colloquialisms?" He pushed Truman's snout out of the way and continued to stare at her.

"Yes." Shannon snorted a laugh. "I saw the look in Deputy Kroeger's eyes. Another house was burglarized. I happen to show up at the scene of another crime. I grew up there. Can you see where I'm going with this?"

Glen scrubbed his hand over his jawline. "I'm genuinely perplexed. I don't see the connection between—"

"Doesn't matter." Holding her breath, Shannon took the exit out of Benton City. "Want to hear my favorite scripture verse?" She didn't wait for his response. "'Therefore, if anyone is in Christ, he is a new creation; the old has gone, the new has come!' From the book of Second Corinthians, I believe."

"I'm impressed." Shannon studied his profile. If he had any questions about her outburst, nothing showed on his face. A class act. "Chapter five and verse seventeen," he said. "Good life verse."

Pop! Boom! Her body started to vibrate with the shuddering steering wheel, and she gripped it hard to control the truck. "Oh no." She felt near tears. "A blowout."

"Pull over." Glen opened the window and waved at oncoming traffic, signaling them to go around.

Of course. She'd been driving on four bald tires since she'd left Walla Walla a year ago. Why today? Shannon pulled onto the shoulder, put the truck in PARK, and jumped out. Glen joined her at the rear of the truck, knelt, and examined the deflated tire.

"It's no wonder." He stood and gave her a look of disbelief, then strode to the front and leaned down. "The tires are threadbare, actually. Do you have any idea how dangerous this is? You need four new ones."

"I don't *want* four new tires." Shannon went to the cab of the truck, reached behind the seat, and began a search for her jack.

"What are you looking for?" Glen pulled his cell from the holder on his belt.

"This!" She held it up as proof that she had everything under control. "I know how to change a tire."

"I'm sure you do, but where is the spare?"

Her triumph died quickly when she was hit with the sickening realization that she'd made use of the spare on her drive from Walla Walla to the Tri-Cities. The tire it had replaced was unfixable.

Glen was chatting on his cell, requesting a tow truck. She paced and felt a strong urge to wring his neck for his take-charge attitude. As he gave instructions to the tow company in his commanding British accent, her agitation increased. Where would she get the money for a tow truck? A new tire?

Glen snapped his phone shut. "That's settled then. They'll be here soon." He replaced the phone into its holder and buried his hands in the pockets of his black wool coat. Then he smiled up at the clear sky. "Cold but lovely day, isn't it?"

Shannon huddled deeper into her corduroy jacket. "Right. It doesn't get much better than this. Are you trying to annoy me?"

He grinned. Then her phone trilled, and she fished it out of the depths of her handbag. "Like a switchboard around here," she mumbled. "Hello?" Shannon inched away from Glen and kept her voice low.

"Shannon, this is Deputy Kroeger."

eight

Poor Shannon. Glen sneaked another peek at her in the backseat of the tow truck, which reeked of cigarettes and stale coffee. Eyes closed, she rested her head against Truman's shoulder. Her vehicle, hooked to the back of the tow truck, looked as pathetic and battle weary as she did. He wished she was leaning against him again so he could hold her tight. He wanted to protect her from everyone, including Deputy Kroeger. The lawman had brought out the same reaction in Shannon today that he had witnessed the last time they'd encountered him. Some sort of fear.

Glen sighed, struggling to make sense of the interplay between her and the deputy. Something about her upbringing and her parents made her insecure. On her own turf at the store, Shannon didn't appear needy or downtrodden. She was the eccentric young woman with silver rings on each of her slim fingers thoughtfully staring out her shop window, a faraway smile on her pretty face and a flower in her golden hair.

The phone call she'd received before the tow truck arrived replayed in his mind. Shannon's face had grown pale as she listened to Kroeger telling her the box was gone. The news was unwelcome but not unexpected.

Glen had no clue what to do next or how they could locate the box. At the moment there seemed no way to stop the approaching train wreck of Amanda's vengeance.

"Got a cigarette?" The tow truck driver slapped his big paws against the pockets of his shirt.

"I'm afraid not." Glen glanced at Shannon again. The morning had been hard on her. He'd like to take her to dinner, as a friendly gesture, but he was meeting Mike Carroll this evening. "How much longer before we get to the gas station?"

"About five minutes. Why? Your girlfriend sick?"

Girlfriend? Did he and Shannon look like a couple? More like Felix and Oscar from *The Odd Couple*. Glen bit back a laugh, but at the same time, he felt good. "No, she's fine. Just a little tired."

"That dog back there bite?" The driver, with RICHIE embroidered on his torn shirt pocket, glanced in the rearview mirror. "I don't like the way it's lookin' at me."

Too bad Shannon had fallen asleep. She would've jumped to Truman's defense, explaining that the dog was not an "it" but a "he."

"Actually, we suspect he's part wolf." Glen felt privileged that Truman was his friend. "But he's harmless. Perfectly harmless."

Richie frowned and moved closer to the door, as if he was about to bail. "Dog bites me, I'll sue."

"Understandable." Glen hid his grin behind his hand. No wonder Shannon had such fun with her wolf tale. She was positively adorable, even if she was a study in contradictions.

"Here we are." Richie pointed in the direction of the gas station on the corner, and disappointment washed over Glen.

He should be pleased that this jaunt with Shannon and Wolf-dog would soon be over, but he longed for more time with her.

In the gas station office, Richie broke the news to Shannon and him that they needed to replace all four tires.

"No." Shannon shook her head. "Just fix the one that's flat." She wouldn't look Glen in the eye, just fiddled with her purse strap.

"He's right." Glen decided to try sound reasoning again. "You can't keep driving on those bald tires. It's only a matter of time before another one goes."

The mechanic jutted his chin toward Glen and wiped grease from his hands on an oily rag. "You keep those ones on your truck, you're gonna kill yourself. I ain't gonna replace just one. It'll be like committing murder or something."

"Um, let me see." Shannon turned her back toward the men, dropped her purse on a table cluttered with old magazines, unzipped her bag, and riffled around inside. Was she looking for her credit card? "What'll it cost? The four tires—"

"I've got it," Glen said and handed the mechanic his card.

Shannon's head snapped up. "No, no, no. You just told me about Thomas and—"

"Forget it."

The mechanic was already swiping the credit card through the machine while Shannon continued to shake her head. "Glen, please, I'll get new tires next month."

"No, we'll get them right now." He signed the receipt, and the mechanic walked into the garage, shaking his head.

She looked on the verge of tears. "Okay, the truth is, I won't be able to pay you back till next month. So please"—she pointed—"tell that man you've changed your mind."

Glen slipped his hands into his coat pockets and walked toward her. "But I haven't changed my mind."

"Didn't you hear what I said?" She released a jagged breath, then pointed to the clock on the wall. "Besides, we're going to be late opening our shops."

"Consider it a loan." Glen shrugged. "I can afford that for now. And we won't be that late." He'd caught on quickly that she was broke, and the thought of her driving on threadbare tires made him feel sick inside.

Shannon opened her mouth, no doubt to protest, but she instead placed her hand on his arm. "Thank you. I. . .just. . . thank you." Her eyes filled with tears.

What matter the cost? To be able to do something to make the flower child's life easier made him happy.

❧

Shannon pulled her truck into her parking space in the alley. Silently all three of them got out of her truck. Truman went off to sniff along the building. Shannon slipped a glance at Glen. His expression was pensive.

"I don't know what to do," she said quietly. "I need to fix this spice box problem."

He blinked. "It's not *your* problem; it's *our* problem."

"You mean it?" she whispered.

He frowned. "Of course. Despite how I came across when Venus first sold the box, I don't hold you responsible for its loss."

Relief washed through her, and a genuine smile came to her face. Glen wasn't accusing her of wrongdoing. Even better, she didn't have to feel alone.

"I still don't know how to find the box, but I know someone who does."

"Deputy Kroeger?" She stared at him hopefully.

Glen smiled. "Possibly, but I'm talking about the Lord." He reached his hand out toward her. "Why don't we pray and ask for the Lord's help?"

Shannon took his proffered hand, and his fingers closed around hers. While he prayed, she asked God's forgiveness—she couldn't concentrate on anything but the warmth of Glen's grasp.

After they were done, they said good-bye twice, then stood awkwardly beside the back door of Glen's shop. "So then," he said.

Hold me, please.

Without warning, Glen pulled her to himself and hugged her tight. "We'll get through this."

After he'd disappeared inside, Shannon walked to her door on numb legs. A real hug. Glen was so strong and handsome. He smelled so good. She opened her shop, snatched the phone from her desk, and dialed. She was suddenly desperate to hear Allie's voice and get her best friend's insight into the situation. She missed living in the same town as Allie and being able to see her regularly. Smiling, she punched in the phone number. By the fourth ring, she was about to hang up.

"Shannon? I'm here." Allie sounded breathless. "You're calling from the store phone and not your cell. I take it you're still worried it's like putting your head in the microwave?"

"Jury's out." Shannon paced with the cordless, smiling. "I didn't wake the baby, did I?"

"No, our Natalie sleeps like a log." Allie gave a contented sigh. "I'm glad you called. I miss you. What's the latest?"

"I think I'm. . ." . . .*in love*. No way to open a phone conversation with her logical friend. Shannon dropped onto the bench behind the counter and drew two long breaths. What if nothing came of this between Glen and her? Shannon shook her head, refusing to dwell on the negative, cleared her throat, and started again. "When you fell in love with Derrick, how did you know it was the real thing?"

"What? Are you in love?" The panicked pitch of Allie's voice made Shannon giggle. "It's impossible. We talked two weeks ago, and you didn't mention anybody. You didn't fall in love in that short span of time, did you?" She paused. "Well, knowing you, anything's possible. I'm surprised you haven't eloped or something."

"Ha-ha. Very funny. And no, not exactly. It's been a long time coming, and yet it happened in a short amount of time." Shannon closed her eyes. Where should she start? She'd been complaining to Allie for months about the British shopkeeper who nagged her all the time. "I mean, it's somebody I've known for a while. I was always attracted—"

"Don't say it. It's the guy who gives you guitar lessons. The one who helped us move you into the shop because he happened to drive by and notice your beat-up guitar. The one with the motorcycle and leather jacket." Allie laughed. "He sounds like he'd be your type even though you say he's got secrets."

"Oh no. It's not Ray. I mean, he's a great guy, but I don't know why you'd think he's my type."

Allie laughed harder. "He's unconventional and also seems

to be a contradiction in personality. Plus he's a musician, that's why."

"Laugh all you want, but it's not him. Ray's like a brother to me." Shannon stood and began pacing again. "So, do you want to guess?"

"Yes. Don't tell me. I like this game." The clang of pots and pans followed Allie's request. "Is it someone you went to school with?"

"Yeah, one of the many who lined up to dance with me," she said sarcastically. "No."

Allie laughed. "Okay then, let me think."

In her mind's eye, she saw Allie multitasking. Thinking, doing chores. The kitchen spotless and her papers in order. Had Shannon not inherited one neat gene? "Are you working on dinner already?"

"Yeah, we're going to have fish tacos tonight. I found a great source of recipes online, and I bought a program for my computer that helps me plan my menus and my grocery lists for a month." More kitchen noises.

Planning meals for a month? Imagine being that organized.

"Is the guy local?"

Shannon stopped chewing the knuckle of her index finger and sighed. "Yes and no. You'll never believe me."

"Yikes, please don't tell me that it's Bozo. He was truly unconventional."

"Bozo?" Shannon frowned. "I don't know anybody by that name."

"The transient guy you allowed to sleep in your store."

"Oh." Shannon laughed. "That was *Bongo*. A sweet soul, just a bit confused. And he wasn't a transient, just temporarily homeless. I let him stay in exchange for painting my office walls. He left some drips, but overall I liked it. Sort of a muted tangerine—"

"Shannon," Allie injected, "you're getting away from the topic."

"Okay, it's not Bongo. And, by the way, he's got an apartment and a job now. He's doing really well."

"Good for him. Now, let me see. Process of elimination. I know it's not the Brit next door. The annoying one who's been haunting you for the past year to—"

"That would be Glen Caldwell." Shannon suddenly felt foolish. She shouldn't have phoned practical, rational Allie. "You know, sometimes people aren't what they seem to be on the outside. Like Venus with her blue-tipped hair. You of all people should know how that is. Remember how you met Derrick?"

"Huh?" Allie's sharp intake of breath told Shannon she'd figured it out. "It *is* Glen Caldwell!" Her tone made Shannon wince. "Oh my heavens, Shannon, if what you've said about him is true, how can you conform to his type? You're. . .well, you're unconventional. You've got your own way of doing things. You're different. In a good way, of course."

Shannon scanned the kitchen. Her mom would love to hear Allie characterize her as "different." The O'Briens were as different as they came. But was she so different from Glen that a relationship was impossible? And what would Glen think if she invited him into her apartment? People like her parents, Ray Reed, Bongo, and Venus didn't give a second thought to the chaos. But Glen. . ."Okay, Miss Know-it-all. Does Derrick love you for who you are, or did he ask you to change before he married you?"

"Good point. I guess we all make compromises to make things work." Allie laughed. Ouch! Shannon stopped pacing, pushed the curtain aside, and stared across at the parking lot. Glen's sleek silver BMW was parked in its usual spot, as was her truck. She didn't need a better picture of their differences. She let the curtain fall and began to tell Allie about the missing spice box, Amanda, and the two trips she and Glen had made to find the box.

"So it was stolen?" Allie interrupted her litany.

"Yes." She went on to explain how Glen had put his arm around her when Deputy Kroeger was there and how he'd paid for her tires. "And when we got back, he held my hand and we prayed about the situation. And Allie. . .he hugged me. . . tight."

"That's interesting," Allie said softly. "Very interesting."

Shannon sighed. "Maybe I made too much of today." She dropped into the fat leather chair. "But I've been seeing another side of Glen lately, not just the guy nagging me about cleaning up my shop. He's also kind and generous."

"Sounds like it." Allie cleared her throat. "And really, there's nothing wrong with cleaning up, right? Look what happened when my mom organized your Walla Walla shop. Business picked up."

Ouch again. A double whammy of irritation and hurt shot through Shannon. "It's not like my shop was a disaster area." She pressed her fist against her forehead and closed her eyes. "I think I'd better get going. Take Truman out for a walk before he has an accident on the floor."

"Are you crying?" Allie's voice was full of regret. "I'm sorry. What did I say? I didn't mean to discourage you. Maybe Glen *is* the one. Maybe—"

"I'm not crying. Just a bit choked up. I am so disorganized and can't seem to get my life together. I feel like such a failure."

"Why? Because you're not perfect? Because God is still working in your life? You know what? Everyone has stuff they have to improve. Sometimes God puts people in our lives to sharpen us—iron sharpens iron. And sometimes He gives us people who complement us and fill the places where we're weak."

Ray had mentioned "iron sharpens iron," too. Maybe it was a sign from God that there was hope for her and Glen. "True," Shannon conceded.

"I'm really sorry," Allie said. "I love you so much, and I

didn't mean to hurt you."

"It's okay, Allie. And I love you, too. It's fine. Give Natalie a kiss for me, and send Derrick my best."

Shannon hung up and leaned back, staring at an old water stain on the ceiling. Her folks had always let her pursue her passionate interests with single-minded purpose. They applauded her unconventional attitude. If she didn't keep things tidy, they laughed and said it was her self-expression. They accepted her no matter what, but they were the only ones. How had that affected her? Perhaps she was too thoughtless about how she impacted other people. She drew a jagged breath. She was having a lot of trouble accepting herself right now. She didn't really fit in. She'd always have to strive for acceptance.

&

The pianist at The Left Bank Café played a haunting rendition of a familiar love song. Glen found his mind wandering to Shannon. His thoughts ran the gamut from fondness to a desire to protect her. Is this what falling in love felt like? He'd had other relationships, but no other woman had made him react so strongly in so many ways.

He checked his coat, then located the table where Mike Carroll sat waiting for him. He would listen to what Mike had to say about leasing more space, but things were iffy right now, particularly because of Amanda. Then he would broach the topic of Shannon. He just wished he'd paid more attention when he signed the petition. He approached the table, his hand extended.

"Glen." Mike stood and shook his hand, looking pleased to see him. "Hope you don't mind, but I ordered us appetizers."

"Not at all." They both sat, and a server appeared. "Sir, may I get you a drink?"

"Sure, I'll have a Sprite," Glen said as the rail-thin waiter switched his attention to Mike. "Another drink, sir?"

"Sure, why not?" Mike drained his glass, then scooted his

chair closer to the table. "Got a call from Amanda today. The woman's livid, I tell you."

Had Amanda broken her promise? Approached Mike with the petition before Monday? "Amanda's livid most of the time, isn't she?"

Mike let loose a congested laugh. "Spunky."

That's not how Glen would describe her.

The server set down their drinks. "Whenever you're ready to order, gentlemen."

"Later." Mike sent him away with a dismissive hand motion. "All kidding aside, the Franklins carry weight in this town. What Amanda wants, Amanda gets."

She must have some kind of hold over Mike. The certainty of his statement deflated Glen's hope, puncturing holes in his plan to appeal to Mike's lighter side. Glen shrugged. "What is it exactly that Amanda wants?" As if he needed it spelled out.

"Besides you?" Mike chuckled and leered at him, and Glen shifted in his chair uncomfortably. "The other thing she wants is what you want, too, Glen. You want Shannon out of the store next to you."

"I never said that."

"Amanda told me you did."

"That simply isn't true. Either you misunderstood her or she lied to you."

Mike shrugged. "That's what she said. Well, she usually does what it takes to get what she wants."

That was a true statement. He was so deep in thought he hardly noticed the server leave a tray of raw clams. Not his thing. "Mike, what do you know about Amanda?"

"Besides the fact that she's rich as Croesus and she wants to invest in my properties?"

There it was. The hold Amanda had over Mike. She had a way of wriggling her way into greedy pocketbooks. Glen huffed out a sigh. "I mean, what do you know about her family?"

Mike shrugged. "Daddy was rich. Other than that, no clue. They aren't from around here. Moved in about ten years ago." He leered again. "You could have her, you know."

"I'm not interested," Glen stated adamantly.

Mike laughed again. "Can't deny, Shannon is a looker. Shape in all the right places. At least from what you can see of her in those weird clothes she wears. Certainly doesn't show off her assets."

Glen clenched his fists to avoid reaching across the table and popping Mike in the jaw. The obnoxious man lifted his glass and waved it at the server, rattling the cubes, then nodded for another. "C'mon, Glen old boy. Dig in." He slurped a clam off its shell, and Glen's stomach did a backflip.

"This is not about Shannon's looks," he said through gritted teeth. "I believe Shannon is open to my assistance at this point. You've got my word that I'll help her fix up her shop, change her sign." He searched Mike's pale eyes. "Whatever you ask."

Mike summoned the waiter with a snapping finger. When he arrived, Glen gave him a subtle, sympathetic shrug.

"I'll have the Chicken Francese," Mike bellowed. He turned to Glen. "What'll you have?"

Glen shook his head. "Nothing. I ate a late lunch." In reality, he'd lost his appetite.

Mike eyed him. "You sure?"

"Yes."

The server slipped away. Glen put his elbow on the table and leaned toward Mike.

"Now, as I was saying, I can work with Shannon."

"I don't know, buddy," Mike said with his mouth full. "Amanda's been talking to all the store owners, and the majority seem to have complaints about O'Brien's shop. I gotta keep my store owners happy."

Glen wondered if they really wanted Shannon shut down or if Amanda had bullied them like she bullied everyone else.

Mike swallowed loudly. "I can make you happy, too. I'm offering you more space to expand. You've got a successful business."

"To expand means someone is moving out," Glen said, sudden dread making his muscles tense. "Do you mean Shannon?"

Mike shrugged and sat back in his chair, looking at him with glassy eyes. "I haven't made any decisions yet about anything. But if something becomes available, are you interested?"

"Probably not at this time." Especially since he suspected it would be Shannon's space. Besides, at the rate things were going, Glen might be out of business as well.

Mike shook his head. "Well, I've got some advice for you. Take it or leave it."

Glen leaned in closer. There had to be a way out.

"Don't let any woman, I mean *any* woman, mess with your head."

That was laughable coming from a man who allowed Amanda to push him around. "That's it?" Glen asked. "That's your advice?"

"Yeah. You're a clean-cut kid. Well, a kid compared to me. You want to get fat and bald and unhappy? Marry the wrong woman." He leaned in closer. "Money helps, you know. A rich woman with long legs and a nice car."

Like Amanda? Glen shook his head and pushed back his chair. "I've got to go."

Mike shrugged. "The deal still stands, at least for a little while."

As he began to leave, a dapper man in a blue pin-striped suit approached the table.

"Ah, William." Mike stood and shook the man's hand. "Glen, this is William Shepherd. He owns this hotel and several others. William, this is Glen Caldwell. He has an antique store in one of my buildings in downtown Kennewick."

William stretched his hand out to Glen. "I've heard the name. You're the British fellow who sells art deco."

"That would be me," Glen said, shaking his hand.

"Pleased to meet you. I have a friend who bought some pieces from you. Exquisite."

"I'm always happy to hear about satisfied customers." Glen offered an appreciative nod.

"Join me for dinner, William," Mike said, waving at the seat Glen had vacated.

Glen took that as his cue to leave, and it couldn't be soon enough. As he retreated across the room, he massaged the back of his neck and tried to block out the sad lyrics coming from the woman at the piano. A song about lovers saying good-bye.

Short of a miracle, Shannon would have to close down her shop. Would she blame him? What were his options? He could appeal to the other store owners, but Mike was ultimately the one to make the decision, and he had already made it, though he hadn't stated it outright. All thanks to Amanda.

Should he warn Shannon? What good would it do now? If she were forced to close her store, she'd move back to Walla Walla. The thought of not seeing her daily made him feel frantic, even when she made him so confused he couldn't think straight. *Lord, I need wisdom, please.*

The song lyrics broke into his thoughts again. Taunting him.

His heart was in trouble. Big trouble.

nine

Shannon pulled into the church parking lot on Sunday morning as the radio announcer warned of high-wind conditions the following evening. Low visibility on the roads was expected due to a probable dust storm. She sighed. One of the drawbacks of living in the middle of the desert.

After she'd exited her truck, Shannon caught sight of Venus getting out of her little Toyota.

"Hey, wait up," Shannon called out.

Venus stopped, and Shannon walked to her and opened her arms wide. The teenager's hug was less than enthusiastic, and Shannon stepped back. "Is something wrong?" She took note of the dark circles under her eyes.

"I didn't feel like getting up today." Venus shrugged. "I was up way too late last night." She shot her a covert glance. "I came like I said to support you, and I also invited some friends. Will that make you more nervous?"

"Not your friends. I'm glad they're coming. But Glen said something about coming, and I told him next week would be better. I don't want him hearing my testimony."

"Huh?" Venus finally gave Shannon her full attention. "I don't understand. You're the one who taught me not to judge people. You accept everybody, and you're worried about Glen accepting you for who you are? If he doesn't, he's not good enough for you. Isn't that what you told me? It's something I'm still working on."

Shannon stared, mute. There was nothing worse than people using her own words against her.

Venus rubbed her foot on the ground. "You've accepted me from the beginning. I hope you always will."

"What? Of course I will." And she meant it from her heart. "Take it from me, you shouldn't crave approval, except from God." Words she needed to apply to herself.

"Sometimes God feels very far away," Venus said softly.

"I know how that is. I usually feel like the odd man out. I think I flaunt my differences just to prove. . ." Shannon shrugged. "I don't know. Just to prove I can? And all my life I've had relationships with people I was positive wouldn't reject me." *Many of them people who were lost and broken.*

"I want Louis to accept me," Venus said, her voice filled with longing. "I'm meeting him this afternoon." She blinked away tears. "I feel like he's going to break up with me."

Louis? Shannon tried not to wince. She had met the boy once and didn't like him much. He was arrogant and treated Venus poorly. But Shannon could see there was a certain "bad boy" appeal to Louis.

"Is he from a wealthy family?"

"Not really." The faraway look returned to Venus's eyes. "He works hard to get nice things."

"Works hard doing what?"

Venus shrugged. "I'm not totally sure. He says he does something with his dad."

"Oh." What exactly would that be, and how well did her employee know her boyfriend?

Venus took a deep breath. "My friends are excited to hear you speak. It'll be good. They'll hear your testimony and realize if you could turn your life around, anybody can."

Shannon managed a smile. "That's good. I hope what I have to say will help them." She had prayed that prayer as soon as she'd agreed to get up in front of the congregation, but the reminder of public speaking brought a stab of nerves that hit her square in the pit of her stomach. What could be worse than speaking in front of a large group?

"You will help them." Venus finally smiled. "You helped me even though I don't deserve it."

"What?" Shannon's concerns fled. "What do you mean you don't deserve it? Of course you do. Everybody does." She pulled at Venus's arm. "Come on. Let's go inside."

As they walked up the front steps, Venus slid a glance at Shannon. "Charlie talks to me a lot. He thinks Glen's got a thing for you."

"Really? Ray says that, too. I'm not sure what to think. I know I frustrate Glen out of his mind. I've caused him so many problems, and we are so totally opposite." She opened the church door for Venus. "I think Charlie's got a thing for you, by the way."

"Charlie?" Venus stopped cold in her tracks and shook her head. "He knows I'm seeing Louis. I mean, Charlie's a really good friend. I can tell him anything. He'd never, ever give away my secrets, but Louis. . ."

Other people walked up behind them, and Venus shoved the door open. Shannon pulled off her Native American wrap. "It's precious that you can entrust Charlie with your deepest, darkest secrets. Don't take that for granted. That's how it is with me and my best friends like Ray and Allie. We tell each other the absolute truth."

"The absolute truth." Venus sighed. "I'll save a seat for you with us on the front row." She gave Shannon a genuine hug and walked away.

Shannon looked around at the congregation gathering. She didn't know most of the members well, but all of them had been kind to her. They would be a good audience. If only she could calm her nerves.

Someone tapped her on her shoulder. Shannon whirled around and found herself looking up into Glen's blue eyes.

"It's you." She sucked in a deep breath.

"Indeed." He looked down at himself, then back at her. "At least it was me when I woke this morning." He felt his face and head with his open palms. "As far as I can tell, it's still me."

"Funny," she said. "What are you doing here?"

"Going to church."

"Yes, I can see that, but I told you not to come today." She wanted to run away, but her legs were anchored to the floor.

"If I recall correctly, you didn't tell me *not* to come today. You *suggested* I come next week."

"Yes, okay. So why didn't you?"

"Why didn't I?" His brows lowered into a frown. "I might come next week as well. Why would it make a difference? You're a little snippy this morning."

As more church members entered, Shannon's nerves felt like twisted rubber bands. Not only was she going to speak in front of a bunch of people, that bunch would include Glen. And today he would hear about her past. She held tight to the paper in her hand with the testimony on which she'd worked for weeks. Breakfast churned unpleasantly in her stomach as she reminded herself that she should be proud of what the Lord had done in her life, not worried that it would turn off a man like Glen.

"Shannon?" Glen said.

She took a deep, cleansing breath and looked up at him. Wasn't Venus right? If Glen really liked her, even as a friend, wouldn't he accept her for who she was? Shannon relaxed a smidgen and smiled. "I'm sorry I snapped. I'm nervous about giving my testimony at the end of the service."

"You're giving your testimony? Really?" His frown deepened. "And you didn't want me to hear it? Is that why you didn't want me to come?"

She nodded.

"I thought we were friends. I even know your secret about reading body language."

Was that hurt in his eyes? "We are friends. I'm sorry. I really am nervous." Shame heated her cheeks.

Glen shifted the leather Bible in his hands. The gold on the edge of the pages was worn, attesting to the fact that the book was well used.

Shannon laid her hand on Glen's arm. "I have to go find the pastor. The service is going to start in about twenty minutes, and we have to pray." She opened the door that led to the sanctuary.

Glen hesitated. "Will you come back to sit with me?"

The plaintive tone in his voice sent a pang of regret to her heart. "I'm sorry. I can't. I have to sit up front, and as far as I can tell, the rest of the front row is taken up by Venus, her friends, and the youth group. But you can sit there." She pointed to an empty seat halfway down the third row.

"All right." He smiled. "Go get 'em, tiger. I know you'll do well." Then, with one more backward glance at her, he walked down the aisle. She watched his retreating back. Though he had smiled at her, a wall had formed between them. Her fault. She'd hurt him by trying to protect her own feelings.

I'm not fit for polite society, she thought as she walked through the foyer and down the hall to the pastor's office. Perhaps she could worm her way out of speaking today. She wanted nothing more than to go home, drink tea, and practice her guitar.

As she raised her hand to knock on the pastor's door, someone clutched her arm. "Shannon, I need to talk to you."

She turned and met the gaze of Yvonne, a young woman who had recently begun attending the church and the niece of Joe, the man who owned the gift shop on the other side of Glen's store. Yvonne helped Joe some weekends, and afterward she'd drop by The Quaint Shop to chat—at least that's what Yvonne called it. Shannon called it gossip, which she despised. She looked around now and wished for a way to avoid a conversation. She didn't need anything else to disrupt her balance.

"I'm sort of in a hurry," Shannon said. "I'm giving my testimony today, and I have to talk to Pastor Zach."

"I'll only be a minute." Yvonne left her hand on Shannon's arm and looked at her with a wide gaze that might have been sympathy. "I was surprised to see you talking to Glen Caldwell."

Shannon frowned. "Why?" Did everyone think he was out of her league?

"Listen, Shannon." Yvonne tugged at her arm to bring her closer. "Amanda Franklin is Glen's best customer."

"I know that," Shannon said.

"That means he'd probably do anything to please her."

Shannon shrugged. "I wouldn't think so."

"I don't think you understand," Yvonne said. "Amanda has it in for you."

"That's not news to me," Shannon said. Where was this going?

Someone called Yvonne's name, and she waved. "Be there in a sec!" Then she turned back to Shannon and leaned close. "Just watch your back. My uncle said she wants to get you shut down. She's doing whatever she can."

"Shut down?" The words stung like a slap to her face. No wonder Glen had been telling her to fix up the shop. Confused, she looked Yvonne in the eye. "Why are you blaming Glen? In his own bossy way, he tried to warn me."

Yvonne huffed out a breath and shook her head. "You're not listening. Glen Caldwell and Amanda are thick as thieves, according to my uncle. That means he must have it in for you, too, don't you think?"

Shannon's breath stopped in her lungs. Was that possible? The look of pity in Yvonne's green eyes, coupled with the surge of irritation toward the gossiping young woman, made her want to run for the nearest exit. She reminded herself to take deep breaths and not allow the young woman's poison to infect her and influence her mind.

Yvonne dropped her hand from her arm. "Just remember, forewarned is forearmed."

Shannon watched as Yvonne sped away. *Like a hit-and-run driver.* Forewarned about what? Seemed to her that the only thing she had to arm was her heart. Still, the damage was done. Yvonne had planted a seed of doubt in her mind. As she knocked on the office door, tears stung her eyes. How would she give her testimony now? Perhaps Pastor Zach and Laurie would let her off the hook.

ten

Glen smiled as he watched Pastor Zach wind up his sermon, arms flying in all directions as he made his final points. The exuberant minister, in his late fifties like Glen's dad, had a similar personality. Enthusiastic, warm, and inviting. Just like Glen's brother, Thomas. Glen knew he could be charming, but he often felt the friendly, warm personality genes had skipped him.

Once more Glen caught a glimpse of Shannon's shining hair, and he felt flat, like a balloon without air. The hurt he'd felt before church when he realized she hadn't wanted him to hear her testimony surprised him. He had known he was attracted to his flower-child neighbor, but his depth of emotion this morning made him realize he was falling in love with her. If only he could be more like his father and Thomas. Warm and expressive. But wishing wouldn't make it happen, and somehow he had to find a way to reach her. Make her trust him. Prove his love. He'd start today by telling her about his meeting with Mike Carroll. Together they would find a solution.

The pastor closed his Bible and smiled at the congregation. "Now we have a special treat for you. We're honored to have Shannon O'Brien give her testimony."

Glen settled back into his seat. Perhaps what she said today would give him better insight into how she'd become the sweet oddity who'd stolen his heart.

"About a year ago, my wife and I saw Shannon sitting way back there." Pastor Zach pointed to the rear of the church to sounds of laughter. Glen smiled, too. "She was forty-five minutes too early for service." More laughter.

That's the early bird, Glen mused, still watching the back of her head.

"With time on our hands, Laurie and I started to chat with Shannon, and well, you know Laurie and Shannon. They kept chatting and chatting." The congregation laughed, and Pastor shook his head. "Then the two continued to discuss a myriad of topics, among them the value of observing body language."

Glen laughed out loud. Shannon was unique. A very special woman.

"Shannon has a heart for the lost." The pastor smiled down at the front row. "And one thing I'll bet most of you don't know is that while Shannon can talk the ears off a mule, she does not like speaking to groups. Go easy on her." He glanced over the congregation and met Glen's gaze. "So without further ado, I'd like to invite Shannon O'Brien to talk about her life."

Shannon stood and walked to the pulpit with hesitant steps. Glen blinked when he saw her dress. He hadn't noticed earlier because of her coat. The pink outfit had to be retro. A throwback to the sixties, but unlike the baggy stuff she usually wore. This dress showed off her figure like nothing he'd seen before, and he had to quickly remind himself he was in church. He forced his eyes back to her face, then noticed the paper in her hand was shaking. Glen had to stop himself from jumping up and joining her at the pulpit to bolster her courage.

Her eyes met his, and Glen smiled. *You can do it, Shannon.* She averted her gaze quickly, nodded at Pastor Zach, and then adjusted the mic to her height. "Thank you, Pastor."

❧

Shannon forced her stiff fingers to straighten her notes on the podium. If she survived this without throwing up, she would never offer to give her testimony again. She raised her eyes and looked out over the congregation of two hundred plus. Big mistake. A sea of eyes focused fully on her. Even the most familiar faces looked foreign in her shaken state.

She glanced at Glen. He nodded and smiled. She wanted to smile in return, but Yvonne's poisonous words came back into her mind. She looked away and ordered herself to focus. Clearing her throat, she repositioned the mic.

"I can't say I'm thrilled to be standing in front of you. Like Pastor Zach said, this isn't in my comfort zone." She swallowed. "And that's putting it mildly."

"You can do it, Shannon!" Venus called out from the front row. The teens next to her hooted and whistled. The chain reaction of laughter that followed loosened Shannon's tight muscles, and she managed a smile.

"I am a walking miracle." She paused, and the reality of the statement hit her like an electric bolt. *It's true. I really am a miracle, and I should be proud of that.* "I grew up not knowing a thing about the real God. If He existed at all, He was whatever a person defined Him—or her—to be." She inhaled. "My parents taught me to respect every religion, every god; meaning, if somebody believed in receiving wisdom from crystals and amulets and that made them feel good, I should go along and join in so I could understand where they were coming from.

"In one way, that was good." She paused to think. "I mean, I learned to love people and accept them for whatever and whoever they are. But while I agree that we need to live at peace with our fellow man, we should not compromise our own beliefs. The thing was, like so many lost souls, I had no real belief system to use as an anchor, so I was plain confused." She caught Glen's gaze again. His smile encouraged her to continue, but she couldn't smile back.

"My parents were true hippies in that era and continued to maintain that lifestyle after I was born. They lived off the land and grew their own food. . .and drugs. Because of their friends and acquaintances, the police—the *establishment*—often paid visits to my house, but things didn't stop. I saw things that no child should see." She swallowed and shoved bad memories from her mind. "When I was six, my dad collapsed on the dirty linoleum floor. Mom wasn't able to talk, so I had to call 911 myself. After that, my father was arrested and jailed for several years. That was a tough time. I blamed myself, but my parents never held it against me. We didn't have much before then, but after my dad went to prison, my mother and I were officially poor.

"According to my mom, fashion and social acceptance was part of how the 'establishment controlled us.' As a result, I didn't buy the latest fashions. I wore hand-me-downs. All the wrong clothes." She stepped out from behind the pulpit and mock frowned. "But now I make a fashion statement wherever I go, don't you think?"

The congregation's spontaneous laughter paved the way for her to finish. "When Dad got out of jail, things didn't improve. He had trouble finding a job. But the good thing was they stopped the drugs. I saw firsthand what the substance abuse did, and it hurt when I couldn't reach my parents in their haze." Warmth washed over her.

"My junior year I gathered the courage to join the yearbook committee. Interestingly enough, the kids there were an eclectic group that accepted me for who I was." Venus's friends were watching her intently. "There was this one kid named Nick who headed up the yearbook committee." Shannon placed her hand over her heart. "A senior with thick dark hair and warm chocolate brown eyes that could melt snow. He was nice to me." She shrugged. "I thought, 'Here we go. He feels sorry for me.' One day he gave me a small Bible, asked me to read it, and said if I had any questions I should call him.

"I started reading the Bible in order to make a list of questions as an excuse to call Nick." The memory was so clear; Shannon smiled to herself. "But in the midst of my reading, my focus switched to Jesus. I believe that's what Nick intended in the first place. I talked a lot to my folks about all of this. They were fine with it. Called it 'cool.' But

I'm still praying that they will come to believe like I do."
She paused. "After Nick graduated, I continued to read my
Bible. I discovered the most awesome truths. You don't have
to clean up your act before coming to Jesus. Even if you're
an outsider in the eyes of this world, standing around in silly
clothes without direction, Jesus wants you to come to Him."

Shannon chanced a glance at Glen. This time his smile
held a touch of sadness. She folded her papers, and Pastor
Zach joined her at the pulpit.

In her relief to be done, she didn't hear much of what
he said, but she exited to another round of applause and
disappeared out a side door. The adrenaline that had given
her energy while she talked was giving way to complete
exhaustion. She didn't have energy left to stay and talk to
anyone. Especially Glen. She grabbed her wrap and purse
from the pastor's office where she'd left them and headed
outside through the back exit.

Giving her testimony reminded her, like she'd said at the
pulpit, that her life was a miracle. Things could have turned
out so differently. So wrong. *Thank You, Lord.*

Hot tears began to stream down her face. She had no
reason to cry, but she couldn't stop. Digging in her purse for
tissues, she took long strides toward her truck. Dark clouds
gathered over Horse Heaven Hills. Cold air snaked its way
under her wrap, chilling her to the core and making the tears
on her cheeks feel like icicles.

As she drove, Yvonne's words wormed their way back into
her mind, attacking like poison darts. Had she imagined
Glen's warmth at church? The hurt in his eyes when he
discovered she hadn't invited him to hear her testimony?

By the time she reached the parking lot behind her shop,
the idea of moving back to Walla Walla brought her a
sense of serenity. She could give Glen an out. Maybe he'd
pound through the wall that divided their shops and expand
Caldwell Antiques. One long, clean line of art deco. Amanda

would watch with a victorious smile. Heat exploded in Shannon's chest, and her hands shook when she thought of Amanda getting her way.

No! She silently berated herself. Anger released toxins in the body, and worse, anger and unforgiveness caused bitterness to take root in the soul.

Shannon leaned back against the headrest, closed her eyes, and breathed deeply. Emotional extremes weren't her norm. She'd lived through enough of those as a kid. She had to do something to get off this crazy roller coaster. Glen. The moment she'd acknowledged to herself that she was in love with Glen, her simple life had become unbearable. Full of fear and uncertainty. Her past had rendered her incapable of a real romantic relationship, and the sooner she departed, the better.

Her desire to go back to the tranquility of Walla Walla deepened. She'd be welcomed there with open arms by Allie, Derrick, and the rest of her friends.

Shannon opened her eyes and stared at her shop across the way. *Too much trouble*, she thought as she hopped from her truck.

She leaned against her back door while she fished her keys from her purse. The door opened of its own volition. Had she left it open? A cold draft sent a hard chill up her spine. She inched the door open while Truman barked wildly in her apartment above the shop. She gasped and froze. Papers littered the floor. One of her desk drawers stood open. Someone had been in her office. . .and they might still be in the shop.

Shannon backed away and spun around. She dug in her purse for her cell phone.

"911, what's your emergency?"

"My store's been broken into."

eleven

After a pleasant chat with Pastor Zach and Laurie, Glen left church with a single-minded purpose—to find Shannon and try to make things right. It would hurt her, but he had to impart his suspicions regarding Mike Carroll's plan to evict her.

She'd be at her shop, hopefully. He forced himself not to drive like a madman through Kennewick. As he pulled into the alley behind their stores, he noticed a police car next to Shannon's rusty truck. Truman was tied outside her shop, whining.

Glen's heart began to hammer. All manner of horrible thoughts went through his mind. Shannon hurt. Shannon scared. Shannon needing him and his not being there.

He cut the engine, jumped from his car, and hurried to the slightly ajar back door. Before he could enter, he heard a man's voice.

"Ma'am, are you sure you didn't just leave the door unlocked? It doesn't look like it's been jimmied. No damage to the lock."

"I suppose it's possible, but that would only give someone easier access. . . ." Shannon's voice trailed off.

Glen knocked and entered. Shannon and a Kennewick police officer turned to face him. Glen's gaze flew to Shannon's pale face. "Are you all right?"

"Glen. Yes, I'm okay." Shannon pointed behind her. "This is Officer D'Amato. He's come to investigate a break-in."

D'Amato jutted his chin in Glen's direction. "And who is this?"

A myriad of emotions crossed Shannon's face. "My friend, um. . ." She shook her head. "I mean, Glen Caldwell, the guy who owns the store next door."

Didn't she consider him a friend? Glen looked from Shannon to the cop. "What happened here?"

"Someone broke into my store."

D'Amato glanced around with slightly raised brows, and Glen sidled over next to Shannon. "What do you intend to do about this?" he asked.

D'Amato shrugged. "I'll make a report, keep an eye out, maybe drive by on my shift, but without any evidence of anything missing, we can't even be sure someone was in here." He turned to Shannon. "You admitted you may have left the door unlocked."

The cop's tone told Glen the most they could hope for was a written report.

"Yes, but Truman was barking his head off. He never barks that way." Shannon sent a pleading glance in Glen's direction.

"That's true," Glen attested. "I've never heard the dog bark continually in the year Shannon's had her shop next to mine. Perhaps one woof when somebody enters."

Shannon turned her grateful smile on him, and his heart soared. Finally he could defend her, for whatever good it would do.

D'Amato closed his notebook. "I'll do what I can." He took a step into the shop, banged into a totem pole, turned, and caught it before it hit a row of brass candlesticks on the floor. "Sorry. That would've caused a domino effect."

Shannon blushed, and Glen quickly looked away from her. The cop was trying to say that the store was a wreck. "Officer"—he cleared his throat—"if Shannon believes someone broke in—"

"Listen, I *know* someone was in here." Desperation rang in Shannon's voice.

D'Amato looked more than a bit doubtful. "Uh, ma'am, I don't want to sound rude, but how could you tell?"

"Shannon has a great memory," Glen said. "She would know how she left things."

"Like whether or not she left the door unlocked?" D'Amato tucked his notebook into his shirt pocket. "Like I said, I'll do what I can." With a nod, he exited through the back door.

"He's not going to do anything," Shannon said bitterly. "And it's my fault. I'm such a slob."

Glen held his tongue. Trying to say anything right now would be navigating a conversational land mine.

Shannon looked up at him, and he struggled with how to comfort her. Perhaps a change of topic would be best. "Your testimony this morning was touching."

Shannon's shoulders dropped. "Yeah, I bet."

"I mean it, Shannon. You reminded me why I need to get closer to God and trust Him."

"That's a blessing, but I imagine you were shocked."

"Why would I be shocked? Everyone has skeletons in their family closets."

"Not like mine. And that was the cleaned-up version," she said quietly. "I didn't reveal all that happened."

"Who says you should have? You are who you are, and that's more than good enough."

"Good enough? What just happened with that cop"—she glanced around the shop—"just goes to prove it."

"Are you serious?" He'd never seen her so discouraged. He took hold of her arms and pulled her close. "Of course you're good enough." His gaze dropped from her eyes to her lips.

"You're kind, but—"

"Shannon." His patience reached the limit. He couldn't resist her anymore. He leaned down and touched his lips to hers softly. She inhaled, and for a moment he thought she would pull away, but she laid her hands on his shoulders and leaned closer. She felt warm and wonderful and alive.

He wasn't sure who ended the kiss, but when they parted, they stared at each other for a full minute.

"I'm sorry—"

"I'm sorry—"

They spoke at the same time, still looking deep into each other's eyes.

"That was unexpected."

"But nice." Shannon pressed two fingers to her lips and stared down at the floor.

His heart pounded. Their relationship had crossed over the friendship boundary, and they could only go forward from here. Going backward was impossible, at least for him.

Shannon began shoving papers around her desk.

Glen watched her with nothing of value to say. "I suppose you should determine if anything was stolen from your shop. If so, you'll have reason to contact the police again."

She nodded, turned, and walked out into the showroom. He followed as she wandered up and down the crowded aisles, looking lost. "I can't tell." Shannon swung around and met his gaze. "That police officer was right. How would I know if something was missing?" She leaned against the counter. "I know someone was in here. I just don't know how to prove it." She stepped behind the counter and opened the cash drawer. "I checked before. There's no money missing."

"You leave your money in the drawer?" he asked.

"Yes." Shannon blushed. "I think this has something to do with the spice box." She narrowed her eyes. "I have no clue why. It's just my gut feeling."

He nodded. "Maybe someone is still looking for it here. Not everyone knows it's been stolen."

"And Amanda is so concerned about recovering it. I know it's valuable, but her behavior is over-the-top, don't you think?"

The thought had occurred to him, but he had pushed it to the back of his mind. "Could be. Perhaps she doesn't believe us when we tell her it's gone. Meantime, why don't you look around and make sure nothing was taken. I'd help, but I wouldn't be able to tell."

"Are you saying my store is a mess like Officer D'Amato insinuated?"

Based on the set of her lips, there was no safe answer to

her question. "I think you're having a reaction to the stress of the break-in."

"I'm having a reaction? What does that mean?"

This was not going well. Glen heard the roar of a motorcycle engine approaching. *Please, not Ray.* He looked at her.

She crossed her arms. "That's Ray."

"I assumed so. Why is he here?" Glen snapped, wishing Mr. Leather Jacket would drive away into the sunset.

"I called him." The roar of the motorbike engine grew louder.

"You called him, and you didn't call me?" What were these emotions boiling through him? He wanted to punch a hole in the wall.

Shannon's glance slid toward him. "Yes, I called him. After I called 911. I...I'm not sure why."

Glen's mind was full of ugly thoughts. "How much do you know about him, anyway?"

Shannon's eyes grew wide, and she slammed the cash drawer shut. "You're questioning Ray?" A breath hissed through her lips. "Are you saying you think Ray was behind this break-in? You've got to be kidding. Are you looking at all my friends as suspects? Venus, too? And will you report all of that to Amanda?"

"Report it to Amanda? What are you talking about?" The rumble of the motorcycle engine died.

"You think all my friends are riffraff. Ray happens to be one of my best friends. Like a brother." She paused and slapped her right fist into her left palm. "Yvonne told me horrible things this morning."

Glen heard the sound of footsteps outside. "I didn't *say* your friends are riffraff. And what about what Yvonne said? Yvonne who?"

"Joe's niece. And I know exactly how you feel about my friends. I wish I could trust you, Glen."

Her last sentence hit him like a rock. "I assure you, I'm quite trustworthy."

The back door swung open, and Rebel without a Cause walked in. Shannon stood with her arms crossed. Glen glanced at Ray, who stopped cold, gaze jumping from her to Glen and back again.

"Okay, talk about your awkward entrances. I take it I interrupted something. I can tell by the cold temperature in the room. Should I leave and come back?"

"No," Shannon said.

"Yes," Glen said.

"All righty then. We've got a classic difference of opinions here." Ray leaned against the counter and crossed his ankles. "Shannon, you okay?"

"Of course she's okay," Glen snapped. "She's with me. Do I look like I'm. . .*not trustworthy* to you?"

"Looks can be deceiving," Ray countered and unzipped his leather jacket. He looked Glen up and down. "Still, you're probably all right."

Shannon snorted, and he turned his attention to her. "You sure you're okay?"

She held up her hands. "I'm fine." She pointedly looked at Glen. "I think he was just leaving."

With every muscle in his body tense, Glen kept his anger at bay and simply nodded. "We can talk later."

"Whatever, Glen." Shannon turned her back to him. "Come on upstairs, Ray. I'll make us tea."

twelve

With no memory of driving back to his apartment, Glen exited his vehicle in front of his apartment building, then slapped the car door closed. How had things gone bad so quickly? One moment Shannon was looking to him for protection and responding to his kiss, the next she openly rejected him—in front of Reed. Not trustworthy, indeed. Glen hadn't even had a chance to talk to her about Mike. Maybe he should just let her find out the hard way.

Glen walked into his apartment and flung his keys on the table in the foyer without a care as to marring the expensive marble top. He pulled off his coat and tossed it on the sofa, then kicked off his shoes and left them as is.

"There you have it. A mess." In more ways than one. If he kept this up, his house would look like Shannon's store. But he wouldn't dare tell her that. He went to the kitchen, opened the fridge door, slammed it shut, and opened it again. He drew a breath and snatched a bottle of orange juice from the top shelf. "And I must stop talking to myself."

He reached into the cupboard and knocked two glasses off the shelf. He watched helplessly as they crashed on the tile under his bare feet, sending shards in all directions. *Just great.* He tried to sidestep the mess to get his broom, but a sliver lodged itself into his big toe. The needlelike pain was nothing compared to the pain in his heart. "Forget it. I'll clean it up later."

After an eternal interval of digging out the long splinter of glass, he bandaged his toe and headed back to the living room. There he dropped on the couch and forced himself to take slow, deep breaths.

Shannon. As his anger subsided, reason returned. Today he realized the extent that he'd hurt her in the past with his comments about her store. And to be fair, today he had questioned the honesty of her good friend, Ray. Whether the man deserved her trust or not, Glen should've expected her reaction. Anyone worth their salt would defend someone they considered a friend.

He tried to ignore the spasm of jealousy the thought of Ray brought, but he couldn't. How had Ray managed to become so close to Shannon? Glen couldn't seem to make any progress at all. No matter how hard he tried, he couldn't get things right. If only the spice box would turn up, maybe Amanda would calm down, and he would be able to charm her and Mike into letting things go with Shannon.

At first glance it appeared the missing spice box had caused all the problems that had arisen in the last few days. But in reality, it had only exposed things that were already bubbling under the surface. Festering sores, like Amanda's jealousy of Shannon and Glen's jealousy of Ray. He had to face the fact that Amanda would probably proceed with her petition whether the spice box turned up or not. The only thing he could hope to gain by the return of the box was possibly to keep Amanda's business. And if it weren't for his brother and Glen's outlay of money for Amanda's last order, he would not be interested in keeping that.

Still, the missing box could bite Shannon. She could be sued. So...were his and Shannon's suspicions warranted? Did the break-in have something to do with the spice box? And why today? The spice box wasn't there—but who else knew that for sure besides himself and Shannon? Nothing made sense.

There was something more at stake than the spice box. What? Art deco was his forte, and spice boxes were from an earlier period. But he recalled the boxes sometimes had a hidden compartment. Was it possible there was something hidden in Amanda's? Something valuable she wanted to recover? Was she behind the break-ins? How could that be possible? She would have had no way to get the addresses of the homes where the spice box had been. He shook his head. That didn't make sense. He propped his feet on the coffee table. "Think," he whispered, not unaware that he was speaking aloud again.

Glen clamped his hands behind his head and squeezed his eyes shut. His thoughts continued to travel back to Shannon's kiss and how it felt to hold her. His fingers itched to pick up the phone and dial her number. As he reached for his cell to call her, it rang in his hand.

He recognized his father's number and quickly pushed the button.

"Dad! Is everything all right?"

"Yes, I just got in. I went to pick Melissa up from the airport. Thomas will be arriving with the children in a week or so after he gets things settled in Haiti. That's what I called to tell you."

"Thank you, Dad. How's Melissa?"

"She'll see a doctor this week."

"I'll be praying."

"I know you will, son." His father paused. "Melissa told me what you did for them. The money, I mean."

Glen sighed. "I didn't want them to tell you." Last thing he wanted was for them to discover he'd borrowed the money.

"I've asked the Lord to bless you for your generosity. Our church will be taking donations for them as well. And we have some friends who are starting a community fund-raiser."

They chatted a few minutes more, then said their good-byes. Glen pushed the OFF button on the phone. At least one thing he'd done recently had turned out well. Now if he could just fix things for Shannon.

❧

After Shannon and Ray drank their tea and ate salads, she

washed the dishes while he sat back in the kitchen chair with his arms behind his head. Truman lay quietly at Shannon's feet. He wasn't nearly so enamored with Ray as with Glen.

"Nice dress," Ray said, pointing at the outfit Shannon had worn to church.

She looked down. "Thank you. Vintage sixties."

"So are you ready to talk now?" Ray asked. "You've been oddly quiet, and for once I got more than a few words in edgewise."

"Ha-ha." Shannon couldn't help but smile.

He tapped his fingers on the tabletop. "Why was the air thick with tension between you and Caldwell when I walked in today?"

She placed the washed teacups in the drainer and turned to face him. "Too many things. Glen kissed me, for one. And he was asking questions about you."

"About me? What kind of questions?"

"He insinuated you might be behind the break-in and wondered how well I know you."

Ray nodded. "Is that such a bad thing? Seems like he's just trying to look out for you, don't you think?"

"Don't you go all bossy and superior on me, too, Ray."

"Bossy and superior?"

"Yes. Like Officer D'Amato who didn't believe me. He kept looking around at the mess and wondering how I could know if *anything* was missing." She rubbed her arms. "What a morning. And I can't believe I let him kiss me."

"The police officer?"

Shannon glared at Ray.

A tiny smile crossed his lips. "Okay, let's talk about the kiss and get it out of the way so I can get you to concentrate on the break-in."

She frowned. "What do you mean?"

"I'm not surprised Glen kissed you. Caldwell looked madder than me when Amanda was outside railing at you.

Hey, my temper has gotten me into trouble in the past, but even I conceded defeat when I saw the look in Caldwell's eyes."

Shannon sighed. "I don't know what to believe anymore. I found out some things this morning." She related her conversation with Yvonne.

"Ignore gossip. It's healthier." He reached across the table and squeezed her face like she was a kid. "Why don't you simply ask Caldwell if it's true?"

Shannon opened and shut her mouth. "I did, in a round-about way. But I was getting too angry. Then you walked into the shop."

Ray's expression grew serious. "So, tell me about the break-in."

"I'll start with everything leading up to it." She shared the events of the past few days. Ray moved closer to the edge of his seat, his eyes alight like she'd never before seen them.

"Two break-ins," Ray repeated, "and both occurred where this box was supposedly located."

Shannon nodded, and her stomach churned. "Just talking about it scares me."

Ray scrubbed his hand over his five o'clock shadow. "How do you know someone broke into your place?"

"Well, for one thing Truman was barking when I got home. Also, stuff on my desk had been moved around and the drawers opened." She paused. "Of course no one else would be able to see that."

"And you say the lock wasn't jimmied?"

"No. But someone who knew what they were doing could do that, right?"

He shrugged. "It's possible. Or the key was stolen from your shop. Or someone who had a key came in. Hey, even I have a key to your shop."

She had to concede the truth to his statement. She had copies of her key all over the place. She'd given it to a number of people, as well as having numerous copies for herself. Since things were always getting misplaced, she wanted to make sure she was never locked out. "I think this had something to do with the spice box."

"Hmmm." He tapped his fingers rhythmically against his leg, and a deep line formed between his brows.

"Gee, you're acting like more of a cop than that D'Amato guy." Shannon laughed, waiting for him to join her, but Ray only frowned harder.

"That was the name of the officer who came?"

She nodded.

"Listen, do you know where Venus was this morning?"

Where had the mellow guitar player gone? "You think she did this? No way. She was at church with me this morning. Ray, I'm not kidding. You're acting all weird on me. What's up with that? I was fishing for a little feedback, but—"

"I'm just thinking." Ray smiled at her, but his demeanor wasn't the Ray she knew. Glen's question about how well she knew Ray flashed through her mind, and she forced it away.

"I think there's something about that spice box. Maybe something hidden in it." She paused, unsure of what she was thinking. "Some spice boxes have hidden compartments. They were used to stash valuables."

Ray stared at her intently. "Valuables, huh?"

"Yes. I hate to be suspicious, but I wouldn't put anything past Amanda Franklin." She met Ray's eyes. She refused to cast aspersions on Ray or Venus. She couldn't possibly be that wrong about the people she cared for. "Do you know Amanda?"

"Not personally. I'm familiar with the Franklin family. I'd never met her face-to-face until she verbally abused me."

"I was just wondering if. . .well, she wants that box back badly."

"You're wondering if she's behind the break-ins, including yours today?"

"If there was a break-in here. I'm even beginning to doubt myself." Shannon leaned toward Ray. "What are you thinking? Why are you acting so serious?"

"It's just that. . ." Ray rubbed his head as though trying to force a thought to the fore of his mind. "You might say I'm interested in crimes." He released a long breath and picked up his guitar, holding it against his chest more like a shield than an instrument. "I read about things like unsolved crimes. Keep files of things." He shrugged. "It's probably nothing." He strummed a few chords.

Shannon identified the tune as "Lyin' Eyes." Would Ray lie to her?

"Anyway, I might talk to a few people." He stilled the guitar strings with his open palm.

"If you talk to Venus, don't accuse her of anything. She feels badly enough that she sold the box."

"Don't worry." Ray lifted his hand. "You know me, Shan. I wouldn't do that." He winked. "I'd best get going, but call me if you need anything. Any hour. Got that?"

Shannon nodded, feeling strangely alone.

Ray's deep frown returned as he stood and placed the guitar on the table. "Keep Truman with you, okay?" He leaned down and ran his knuckles over her head. "Hey, knucklehead, if the Brit kisses you again, I say go for it."

Shannon blushed, and Ray laughed. He turned and left, boots clumping down the stairs. "I'll lock the door behind me," he yelled up to her.

She peered out her kitchen window that looked out over the back alley. Ray mounted his Harley and drove away. Truman stood beside her, whining, and she dropped to her knees and hugged him. "I'm glad you're here. You aren't confusing at all like everyone else."

Shannon was filling Truman's water bowl in the kitchen when she heard another vehicle pull into the alley and jumped to her feet. Maybe it was Glen, returning to talk to her. She peered out the window again, and her heart beat faster. Not Glen, but Amanda. As she stepped from her car, Shannon searched her own heart. What was it about Amanda that made her feel like a bag lady? Probably because everything about her was expensive and classy, like the fur coat that billowed around her leather high-heeled boots as she headed toward Shannon's back door.

Shannon twisted the rings on her fingers, then straightened her shoulders, brushed imaginary lint from her dress, and headed down the stairs.

She opened the door wide, and a cold breeze rushed past her, shuffling papers on her desk. "I saw you coming. Does Glen know you're here?"

"Glen? Why would he know I'm here?"

Amanda looked Shannon up and down, but she made no move to shove her way in, and Shannon didn't invite her. Behind Shannon, Truman growled low in his throat.

"Why are you here?" she asked.

"I want my spice box back."

Just like that. No niceties. No hellos. "I don't have it," Shannon said.

"You don't have it, or you're just not giving it to me?" Spittle gathered in the corner of Amanda's mouth. "How could you find anything in that rat's nest you call a store?"

Shannon tilted her chin. She refused to be intimidated. "You can ask Deputy Kroeger of the Benton County Sheriff's Department. He's aware it's missing."

Amanda gasped and backed up a step, nearly losing her balance. "You got the police involved without my permission?"

"Your permission? Why would we need your permission? He was a deputy investigating the break-in at the house from where the box was removed."

"You're telling me the box is gone?"

Oops. Shannon had let the cat out of the bag. Glen hadn't told Amanda yet. Big mouth.

Amanda hefted her expensive leather bag on her shoulder. "If I don't get that box back, losing your business will be the least of your worries." Before Shannon could answer, Amanda whirled on her heel and stalked away.

Losing her business? Was Amanda threatening her? Fear trickled down her back. She shut the door and sank down onto her squishy leather chair. She wasn't the only one who was scared, though. Amanda was terrified. There was definitely something about that box that scared her. And why was Amanda here today, asking about the box, when she'd given Glen until Monday to find it?

Shannon tapped her head with her fist. She needed to go somewhere to think—to be alone with God. And she knew where she could do that. The place she'd gone many times when she was young.

thirteen

Shannon's battered truck was parked in its usual place when Glen pulled into the alley. His first reaction was to go rushing into her store, yank her into his arms, and kiss her soundly. But given their last conversation, she'd be more likely to haul off and slug him than to welcome his advances.

He walked into his office, dropped his briefcase on his desk, then went into the showroom where he greeted Charlie with a weary wave.

"Thanks for opening the shop today."

"I'd rather be here than at school."

"Have I gotten any calls?"

"No calls."

"Not even from Amanda?" Glen had expected her to be on the phone nagging him today.

Charlie shook his head. "No, she hasn't called." He grabbed a cloth, turned his back, and got to work dusting.

Frowning, Glen studied him for a moment. Charlie was edgy lately. Could it be that Venus wasn't responding to his overtures? Glen opened his mouth to ask if he wanted to talk, but his cell rang. He yanked it from his pocket and looked at the number on the display screen. It was Amanda. As if mentioning her name had made her call.

"Hello," he said as he walked back to his office.

"I'm calling to give you one more chance." The tone of her voice was chilly.

He sat in his chair asking the Lord for wisdom. "One more chance for what?"

"I want that box, and I want it now."

Glen felt all the frustration of the last week bubbling in his

121

head. "I don't have it. It was stolen. What can I do?"

"Shannon told me you'd talked to the police about the box."

"What? When did you talk to Shannon?"

"Our business relationship is over, Glen. I want my money back. I will arrange for my credit card company to take back my payment."

Glen lost his battle for civility. Amanda's games wearied him. He was sick and tired of being beholden to her. Tired of the way she treated Shannon. "As far as I'm concerned, our relationship is over already. It was over when you broke your word to me. You told me you'd wait until today to talk to Mike about Shannon. But when I met with Mike Friday night, I discovered you'd already spoken with him."

The empty air between them made him wonder if Amanda had hung up.

"I'm not going to apologize," she barked. "This is your fault. Your fault for encouraging that. . .person next door. Don't expect any sympathy from me. And what if I had waited to talk to Mike till today? Would you have been ready to hand over the box?"

"We don't have the box. And Mike has nothing to do with that. You're not making any sense at all." For the first time in his life, Glen wanted to pick up something heavy and break a window. "I have to wonder what's so valuable about that box that you are ready to sever relationships and punish the innocent."

She gasped. "This conversation is over."

As the phone clicked in his ear, Glen knew for certain that he and Shannon were right. Amanda wanted the box for more than just its antique or sentimental value. He sighed. He had burned the bridge between himself and Amanda, and oddly enough, he felt a great sense of relief. Not that there was any logic to that feeling. He'd lost his best client, and he needed the money. *Lord, I need a miracle. I'm trying to do the right thing. Please bless my efforts.*

Now a new worry nagged at him. How far would Amanda go to protect whatever secret the box held?

Glen pushed to his feet, fueled by urgency to find Shannon. He went to the back window and peered out at the parking lot. Shannon's truck was no longer in its usual spot. He grabbed his coat, poked his head into the showroom, and called out to Charlie. "I'm going next door."

Charlie looked up from dusting and stared, as though his mind were a million miles away. "Is this about the spice box?"

"Sort of." Glen headed for the front door, stopped, and called over his shoulder. "If I'm not back before closing time, please lock up."

Charlie nodded, and Glen exited, hurrying next door.

He stepped into Shannon's shop, and Venus spun around and gasped. "Oh, Mr. Caldwell, I nearly had a heart attack. You know someone broke into the shop on Sunday."

"Yes, I heard all about that." Glen tried to smile. "Sorry I frightened you."

"You didn't exactly frighten me, it's just that I'm jumpy, that's all."

Whatever that meant. He looked more closely at the girl. Her eyes weren't as sparkly as normal and seemed sunken in her eye sockets.

"Are you all right, Venus?"

She blinked and clasped her hands together. "I'm fine—why? Why would you ask?"

"Just that you. . .well, no matter. Just being polite."

"I'm fine." She looked everywhere but at him.

"All right then, I need to find Shannon. Do you know where she is?"

Venus sucked in a breath. "She left a few minutes ago with Truman. She won't be back till tomorrow."

"Tomorrow? Where did she go?"

Venus rubbed her hands over her spiky hair. "I—I don't know if I'm supposed to tell anybody where she went."

"Why not?" Glen had a strong desire to take Venus by the shoulders and shake the information out of her. "Shannon didn't go in search of that spice box again, did she?"

"Um, no. Not that. No."

"Listen to me," Glen said. "You must tell me where Shannon went. I'm worried about her safety." After all the unusual activity surrounding the spice box, he'd reached his breaking point. He had to see Shannon and know for himself that she was safe.

"Her safety?" Venus chewed her fingernail.

Another thought occurred to him. "Is Shannon with Ray Reed? Is that it?" Holding his breath, he waited.

Venus wagged her head. "No way."

"Please."

"Well, okay then." Venus twisted her slim fingers. "She went home. To her parents' house. To hike in the mountains." The words tumbled out of her mouth. "But I wasn't supposed to tell. Shannon wants to be alone. She's been through a lot."

Her narrow-eyed perusal indicated that she thought he was partly the cause of Shannon's problem. She was probably right, but he chose to ignore the silent communication.

"Where's home?" he asked gently. "I know her family is from Benton City, but I need the address."

Venus studied him for a moment, sighed, then went to the counter and scribbled down an address.

"If she fires me for doing this, will you promise to give me a job?"

Glen inhaled and realized what he'd asked of the girl. "If I am financially solvent after all of this is resolved, and if Shannon suddenly becomes someone other than herself and fires you for caring about her, then yes. I will give you a job."

"Thank you," Venus said. "Now I know you really love her."

He wasn't sure he followed her logic, but she was right about his feelings for Shannon.

He thanked Venus for the address, hurried to his car, loaded the information into his GPS, and headed toward Benton City. He tried to call Shannon's cell, but instead of ringing through, it jumped right to voice mail. She had her phone turned off. At least she'd taken Truman with her.

"Lord, protect Shannon from all harm. Please."

Amanda wouldn't send somebody to cause bodily injury. . . would she? Glen's heart sped. He couldn't answer his own question.

fourteen

After a long trek around town that included a hike along the Yakima River, Shannon arrived back at her parents' double-wide, trailed by Truman whose tongue hung from his mouth. The ache in her muscles from the strenuous hike felt good. She savored the cold air against her skin. The wind was picking up, the prelude to the dust storm.

"Let's sit." She dropped to the ground next to an arthritic oak tree in the backyard and snuggled up against the dog. The exercise had been exhilarating, but it hadn't cleared her head like she'd hoped it would. So many issues crowded her mind, and they were intertwined in each other, like wheels within wheels.

She was losing her shop. After her confrontation with Amanda, she knew it was inevitable. That fact should be upsetting her more, but it wasn't. She'd be relieved to have the drama over with. Now other issues were at the forefront. Amanda was the most threatening of all. What if Amanda sued? Even with insurance, that would be a financial disaster. Shannon shivered. There was something about Amanda that gave her the creeps.

And what about Ray? Why had he suddenly changed so? Was Glen right? Was there something odd with Ray? Shannon shook her head. No, not possible.

She closed her eyes and sighed. She had to look at the bright side. Perhaps by leaving Kennewick, she could regain her self-confidence and return to the person she'd been in Walla Walla. She would leave behind most of the things that bothered her so much, including having a shop next to Glen's.

Glen. Everything always came back to him. Truth be told, she didn't want to leave, but maybe they would have a better chance at love if she weren't next to him making his life miserable. Her heart squeezed in her chest. How had her feelings for him spiraled so out of control? She'd had a thing for him since the day they'd met, but now it was like her mind shut down and her heart had taken flight on its own. And that kiss. She touched her index finger to her lips. She'd never felt that much emotion in her entire life.

She took a deep breath and stared upward. White clouds raced each other across the blue sky. She drew her knees to her chest, wrapped her arms around her legs, and bowed her head. "Lord, please give me guidance. I will do whatever You will for my life."

Truman plopped his head against her shoulder and whined.

"I know, buddy. You love Glen, too. But how can it be? Can you imagine what he'd think if he saw this place?" Shannon got to her feet and brushed dirt off her pants.

Her mother's flock of scraggly chickens scattered at her movement, running pell-mell in all directions, just like her emotions. Truman whined again.

"Yep, I know you're thirsty." She filled his bowl next to the trailer with water from her bottle.

The sound of a car engine drew her attention from her morbid thoughts. Who would be visiting her parents? Hopefully Deputy Kroeger wasn't making good on his promise to come by. Shannon hurried around the corner of the trailer, leaving Truman slurping water. She caught her breath and skidded to a stop. The sleek silver BMW rolled to a stop, and Glen exited his car, smiling.

"Glen! What are you doing here?" This was worse than Deputy Kroeger. She wanted to sink into the ground. She wasn't ready for him to see where she had grown up. She'd wanted time to warn him. But, she reminded herself, this might be a good test. Would he look down his nose at her?

"I can explain," he said just as Truman rounded the corner behind her. Without warning he went ballistic, bounding toward Glen at a full gallop. Shannon opened her mouth to tell Glen to brace himself, but didn't have time. Truman pounced, and Glen went down hard, ending up on his back with the dog on top of him.

"Truman, no!" Shannon ran to Glen's side and tried to shove the excited dog aside. "Back off, Truman. Sit!"

The dog glanced at Shannon, then back at Glen.

"Sit, Truman," Glen said.

Still panting, Truman backed away and obeyed.

"He won't even listen to me anymore when you're around," she griped. "Are you okay?"

Glen groaned dramatically and eyed her from under half-closed eyelids. "I think I dislocated my back."

For some reason, all her fears and worries melted away. "No you haven't, you big baby. You deserve that after all the trouble you've been."

"Trouble? I've been trouble?"

"British invasion." Shannon held out her hand. "Now get up." He grabbed her hand, but as she tried to haul him up, he pulled her down, and she landed on her side next to him. Two chickens cackled as they ran past. Truman licked Glen's ear, and he shoved the dog's head away.

"You deserved that," Shannon said, straightening his glasses.

"Indeed. And now I want to apologize for anything and everything I've done to make you mad at me. And anything and everything I will ever do."

"Anything and everything, you say?"

"Yes. Absolutely."

He still held her hand, and he made no effort to let go or to move. She savored the warmth of his touch.

"All right," she said. "Is that why you're here? To apologize?"

"Partially. I need to tell you that I saw Mike last Friday night and he—"

"Wants to kick me out of my store?"

"You knew about that whole thing?"

"Sort of put it all together after Amanda visited me." Shannon's heart felt light. Glen wasn't hiding anything from her. Ray was right that she shouldn't have listened to Yvonne's gossip.

"She did what?"

"I was planning to come back and tell you. I let it slip that the box really is missing. And I also told her that Kroeger knows, and she totally overreacted to that."

He pushed a strand of hair off her face. "That's what worries me and why I'm here. I don't know why she's so frantic."

Shannon felt the warmth of his care. "Thank you for that, but you could have called me." She patted her cell phone in her pocket.

"It's turned off," he said.

She yanked it out of her pocket. "Oh that's right. I didn't want to be bothered."

He took it from her and turned it on. "Give me your word that you won't turn it off again until all this is over."

"Okay. I promise." His worry was contagious, yet it felt so good to know he cared. "Why were you worried about me?"

"Too many break-ins. Then I talked to Amanda this morning and she's—"

"Threatening us," Shannon finished.

"Yes. You're finishing my sentences today."

She stared down into his blue eyes—she could get lost in those eyes. Then she waved her hand in a wide, sweeping motion. "This is how I grew up. In a rusty trailer, surrounded by chickens and a chaotic mess. I was so scared for you to see it all."

"Come here," he whispered as he put his other hand around her neck and gently pulled her toward him. "I like you for you. I don't care how you grew up or where you came from."

Her lips had just brushed his when the door to the trailer

squealed open. Shannon jerked away from Glen and turned in time to see her mother step out onto the rickety wooden deck that ran the length of the trailer. Five cats followed her out the door. Her feet were bare, even in the cold weather.

"Wowzers, look at you kids, playing in the dirt." Mom laughed. "Hey, don't let me interrupt you. Shannon's father and I have been known to—"

"We're not playing, Mom. Truman knocked him over, and I'm helping him up."

"Call it what you want to. That's cool." Mom laughed again.

Shannon hopped to her feet, and Glen followed suit, although at a slower pace, rubbing his back.

"Shannon, baby, where are your manners?"

Shannon huffed out a breath. "Glen, this is my mother, Lois. Mom, this is Glen Caldwell."

Glen brushed off his hands, walked over to the deck and up the stairs, circumventing pots of dead flowers, and held out his hand, but Mom ignored it and gave him a warm hug instead.

Shannon watched, unable to move, fighting total embarrassment. What was Glen really thinking?

"Lois, it's my pleasure. You two look like sisters," Glen added.

"Hear that, Shanny-girl?" Mom smiled her way. "We look like sisters."

"I agree, Mom."

"Why don't you both come inside?"

"Mom—" Shannon felt panic clutch her stomach. What would Glen think when he saw how they lived?

"I think it's a brilliant idea," he said.

fifteen

Glen followed Shannon and her mother through the front door, right into the living room. Shannon's demeanor had changed like lightning, and he thought he knew why. He scanned the shabby, cluttered room and the dish-piled kitchen sink and counters, then caught her watching him. She averted her eyes. She hadn't wanted him to see the mess.

Shannon's cell phone began to trill in her pocket, and she pulled it out and answered it. "Excuse me," she whispered and left the room.

"So, Glen, have a sit down," Lois said. She looked around, then laughed. "Oops, it might help if I clear off one of these chairs." She began flinging magazines and papers to the floor.

Shannon returned with a backpack slung over her shoulder. "I have to go."

Lois straightened and stared at her daughter. "Why, sunshine?"

Shannon met Glen's gaze. "Venus called. She's sick."

"She didn't look well when I saw her this morning," Glen said. "Would you like me to drive you?"

"No, that's fine."

"Glen can visit with me for a little while," Lois said.

Glen was loath to let Shannon go off on her own, but good manners dictated he at least be polite and stay for a little while.

"Please keep your phone charged and on," Glen said.

"Okay," she said as Glen followed her to the door and brushed her shoulder with his hand. Her muscles were tense.

"You can kiss her good-bye," Lois chirped. "Kissing is good for the soul."

"Mom!" Shannon shut her eyes and groaned.

131

Glen laughed, leaned over, and kissed Shannon's head. "Please be careful," he whispered. "And don't worry. I think your mother is charming."

He sensed some of her tension leave, and her lingering look made him feel warm to his toes. "Thank you, Glen."

"Baby doll, you be careful. The wind is picking up, and you know how those dust storms are."

"I will, Mom." She snapped her fingers at Truman. "Come on, boy. Let's go."

He watched until she was in her truck; then he turned to face Lois.

"Sit. Make yourself comfy."

Glen dropped onto the threadbare sofa. "I'm sorry I came unannounced."

She waved her hand. "The best kinds of visits are unexpected." Lois struck a match and brought two candles to life. "My Shannon. She's special, you know."

The candle scent drifted past his nose, and Glen fought the temptation to float off to sleep. "It's been quite a day. Exhausting really."

"I saw stress written all over your face. Shannon's, too. That's why I broke out the candles. Lavender. A scent to soothe the soul," she said with a smile.

Lois's skin, weathered by the sun, didn't hide her fine bone structure and beautiful features. "Yes, soothing, thank you."

"Make yourself at home. You need something to eat?"

"No, thank you," he said hurriedly. Lois might cook like Shannon—bean sprouts and tofu. Not that there was anything wrong with veggie food, except that he disliked it intensely.

Lois pulled up a chair, then sat. "How long have you known Shannon?"

"A little over a year. Since she opened her shop, actually, which is next door to mine." If Shannon had told her mom anything about their relationship, it didn't show on Lois's tranquil face. Her smile remained, and she nodded.

"And how long have you two been in love?"

Her expression didn't change a bit. Was she serious, asking such a personal question? Glen continued to stare at her, mute.

Lois's smile softened. "Okay, that's cool. You'd rather not say." She shrugged. As she watched him with the same disarming hazel eyes as Shannon's, he knew she saw right through his detached facade. He wasn't sure why, but he suddenly felt the need to talk.

"I don't know when it happened or how it happened. One minute we were at each other's throats, figuratively speaking, and then—"

Lois slapped her hand on the crowded coffee table, and Glen jumped. "That's adorable. Isn't that always the way? John and I met in Berkley." She pointed over her shoulder. "John's got a job interview," she said. "Too bad you can't meet him. Anyway, back then his hair was way down past his shoulders, and I was still a snob from the East Coast." She sighed, a faraway look in her eyes. "But he finally got to me. Had me questioning my focus on the material things in life. And politics?" She waved her hand. "I didn't give a hoot about that till John woke me up." Lois shook her head. "I just love that man," she said as though she couldn't help herself.

He found himself wishing he could be as transparent as Lois. Acceptance emanated from the woman, filling the room thicker than the lavender scent coming from the candle. No wonder Shannon was a loving soul. "So then, you think there's hope for opposites, do you?" He looked at her expectantly.

She gazed at him for a long moment. "I know what you want. You want love to be logical, right?" She laughed. "You've got a lot to learn, Glen Caldwell. That's what head over heels means. Kind of like losing your mind. Losing your heart. Taking risks and jumping off cliffs."

"Even when one should know better."

"Yes! Especially when one should know better." Lois moved to the very edge of her seat. "Or it's not true love." She took a deep breath and squinted at him with intensity. "It's like Truman. He doesn't do the math. He sees you, wags his tail, licks your face. . .maybe even knocks you to the ground. He's thrilled just because you walked into the room. That's how love should feel."

Lois's roundabout conversation sounded so much like Shannon, Glen wanted to smile. He could make the argument that they weren't simple animals, but Lois was on a roll, and he didn't want to contradict her.

"I'm not suggesting we're dogs, if that's what you're thinking."

She was as perceptive as her daughter. He laughed. "That's precisely what I was thinking." He smiled at the gentle woman sitting in front of him.

"Do you believe like my Shannon?" Lois asked, catching him off guard.

"What do you mean?"

"The Bible?"

"Yes," he said.

"That's good. That's very good." She nodded her head gently, and her gaze became distant. "Lately John and I have been reading a Bible and. . ." She stared directly at Glen. "Sometime we must have a talk."

"I would like that very much. I—" His cell phone rang. "Excuse me," he said.

"Oh, you go on," Lois said. "But using those contraptions is like sticking your head in a microwave."

So that's where Shannon got her theories. He laughed and glanced at the screen. No number was displayed, but he decided to answer just in case. "Hello."

"If you want the box, follow my directions to the letter."

sixteen

After seeing Venus off with some aromatherapy oils to inhale, Shannon settled at the store counter with a mug of herbal tea, munching a handful of almonds and raisins. Almost closing time. Things were slow today, no doubt because of the weather. The wind had picked up, and the predicted dust storm was beginning. But nothing could diminish the slightly giddy happiness she felt as she thought of Glen on the ground, Truman's seventy-eight-pound body hovering over him, and then the almost kiss. He had come because he was worried about her. She was tempted to call him on her cell phone to ask if he had finally escaped her mother's hospitality.

Amazing that things could go from bleak to hopeful in such a short time. And all because of an almost kiss. No, it wasn't the kiss; it was because she knew for certain Glen cared.

Six o'clock. Time to shut things down. She locked the front door, counted the cash drawer, then walked back to her office. Headlights winked in the alley, and she went to the window and stared out through the cold pane. Hard to see in the dust driven by the wind, but it looked like Glen was back. She was going to see him. She wanted to finish that kiss.

Pulse racing, she ran upstairs to the bathroom with Truman close on her heels. She brushed her teeth, fixed her braid, then swiped on lipstick.

"You be a good boy," she said to Truman before closing her apartment door. She ran out her back door, hesitating only a second to ask herself if Glen would interpret her visit the wrong way. No, why should he? He started it.

She raised her fist to knock when the door flew open. Glen

stood there with a deep frown on his face, holding a briefcase. "Shannon, I'm glad you're here. I was going to call you."

Shannon lost her smile. By the look on his face, she knew she wasn't going to get her kiss now. "What's wrong? Amanda again?"

Glen shook his head. "Not Amanda. I don't want to scare you, but I received an anonymous call. The man told me to meet him this evening at Columbia Park. He's got the spice box."

"What?" Shannon pressed her hand to his arm. "That means it's not Amanda?"

He shrugged. "Not unless she wants money and she's been bluffing. I guess anything is possible."

"You're not going, are you?"

"I am. He'll give me the box in exchange for three thousand dollars. And we'll be done with this, once and for all." Glen's voice was matter-of-fact and void of emotion.

"And you believe him?" Shannon shook her head. "You're not thinking straight. He'll take your money and run. You'll be out three thousand dollars and still have no spice box to show for it. Or worse, he'll hurt you first, then take it all. I don't blame you for not calling the police, but in this case it might be best." She took a deep breath. "This is insane. Our roles have reversed. For once I'm being sensible and you're acting crazy."

"I have to go alone. He—he made a threat against you."

"Against me?" Shannon held her hand to her thudding heart.

"If I called the cops, he warned he would hurt you." Glen cupped his hand around the back of her head and pulled her to him. He kissed her hard, then backed up. "I came here only to get the money from my safe. Please go up to your apartment and lock the door. You've got Truman to protect you."

"How can I let you go alone when I started all this trouble?" Panic swelled her throat, and she had trouble swallowing. What if something happened to him? Looking into his determined blue eyes, she knew beyond a shadow of doubt that she loved him with all her heart. She couldn't bear the thought of losing him. "No, Glen. There's got to be a different way."

"I'm going." He rubbed her upper arm, but Shannon stepped away from him.

She had to think fast to get the information she needed. "At the park? You mean the entrance to the park? Or are you supposed to roam the park all night and wait for him to show?"

"I'm not stupid enough to answer your questions. You'll come to the park after me."

She cut him a defiant look and decided to use a different tack to stop him from going through with this madness. "You can't afford to lose three thousand dollars, Glen. You told me your brother—"

"Look, I must go. Please, I'm doing this for both of us." Glen pulled her into his arms for another quick kiss, then skirted around her and walked to his car. "Go back inside, please."

Glen said something she didn't quite hear as she dashed back inside and began to dig through her desk drawers. "Flashlight... flashlight. There it is!" She held it up in triumph. "C'mon, Truman, we've got a job to do."

After Glen had left the alley, she rushed to her truck with Truman, started the engine, and headed to the park. "Lord, protect Glen. I trust You to protect him. And help me."

Truman *woofed* his agreement, just as Shannon caught the dim sight of the taillights of Glen's BMW through the beginnings of the dust storm. "Thank You, Lord," she whispered as she picked up her cell phone and dialed Ray. He didn't answer. All she got was his voice mail, and she left a message.

&

Glen killed the headlights. He'd been instructed to park at the Kiwanis building, go around back, and leave the briefcase. What was he doing here, in a dust storm, in the pitch-dark in Columbia Park? This was foolish—very foolish. Shannon was right—he should have phoned the police, but the caller had threatened Shannon's life and Glen had made a snap decision to be the hero. Some hero. He cut the engine and tried to visually scan the area, but he couldn't see much through the blowing dust.

He comforted himself with the thought that whoever had the spice box only wanted money in exchange. At least, he prayed that's all they wanted. He grabbed the briefcase off the passenger seat, felt for the flashlight in his coat pocket, and stepped out of the car.

"An even trade," Glen muttered. He flicked on the flashlight and ventured toward the building slowly. An eerie feeling washed over him. He imagined the thief watching him.

Glen drew a breath and stopped in his tracks. This was madness. But he refused to turn back now. Possession of the box meant at the very least that Amanda might reconsider, leave Shannon in peace, and he'd be free to pursue the woman he loved. That is, if Amanda wasn't behind this. Or if he didn't die in the process.

Memories of the caller's words rattled around in his head. "Drop the money on the ground behind the building, then get back in your car. Return in five minutes," he'd said, "and you'll find the spice box behind the building."

The wind howled and blew dust in his face. Glen stopped to wipe grit from his mouth and nose and fumbled with the flashlight. He adjusted his eyeglasses and advanced. The beam from the flashlight did very little to illuminate his way.

When he reached his destination, he did as he'd been instructed and dropped the briefcase. It landed with a dull thud. His fists clenched as he fought the urge to pick it up again and forget the whole deal. *It's for Shannon. Not only will this keep her from danger, but this might make life easier for her.*

He rounded the first corner of the building and heard heavy footfalls behind him. He broke into a jog. *Glen, you were stupid for coming out here. Shannon was right.*

The footfalls came faster. Glen began to run. When he reached the car, he yanked at the door handle.

"You've got your money," he said over his shoulder. "Now keep your word and give me the box."

He heard heavy breathing close behind him as he fumbled to open the car. *It's too late. Shannon was right.*

Then a dog barked. Someone yelled. . .Truman?

The person behind him said something inaudible. Glen glanced over the roof of his car. Through the dust, the beam from a flashlight bobbed. The dog barked again, close enough to hear its panting. A familiarly shaped shadow shot around the front of the car and ran past him.

Glen swung around to watch. "Truman?"

The thief took off running, Truman right behind him.

"Glen?" He whirled at the sound of Shannon's voice. "Glen, are you all right?" She skidded to a stop, but not before she nearly knocked him down.

He grabbed her shoulders to keep them both standing. "What's wrong with you?"

"I was worried about you. I just—"

A deep bellow came from behind the building. Truman barked and growled.

Glen glanced that direction, then back at Shannon. "Go to your truck."

"But I only want to—"

"Now! For once, listen to me, Shannon. You could be hurt."

A shout and yelp followed, and Shannon clutched his arm. "Do you hear? Truman's got the guy."

Truman appeared and rushed toward them. Glen aimed the flashlight at the dog. A bloody piece of sleeve hung from his jaws.

"Truman!" Shannon fell to her knees. "You're such a good boy."

"Stay put," Glen ordered. "I'm sure all is lost. Truman must've scared the guy off."

Glen ran back behind the building, then shined the light at the ground. He saw it—the briefcase and a clear plastic bag beside it. The money. . .and the spice box?

Glen snatched them both and hurried back to Shannon and Truman.

seventeen

Glen placed the spice box on the desk in Shannon's office. Truman sat at his feet, and Shannon hovered behind him. The grit in his mouth, nose, even in his ears didn't improve his mood. "You totally disregarded everything I said." He stared down at her, still furious.

Shannon fisted her hands on her hips. "You'd probably be dead if I hadn't *disregarded* your instructions. Truman saved your hide."

"You don't know that for certain."

"Fine. You wanted to protect me; I wanted to protect you. Let's leave it at that."

"It's just—just not right," Glen stuttered. She was insufferably stubborn. And brave.

She reached up, kissed him full on the lips, then backed away smiling. "That's nice."

He had to agree. His anger was quickly slipping away.

"Okay, let's argue later," she said. "Right now I want to test a theory of mine."

"And that is?" Staying angry with her was impossible.

Shannon slipped around him and began fooling with the box. "Many of these boxes have hidden compartments."

Glen watched her remove the bottom drawer and reach her hand inside.

"If I'm right, there will be a little button kind of thing in here that will release the back cover." She frowned in concentration, then a grin lit her eyes. "Aha, there it is." She turned the box around, dragged it to the edge of the desk, and slid the back off. "Look. Right here at the top. A secret drawer."

141

Glen leaned over to look. Sure enough, it was a drawer, and the inside was filled with cotton.

Shannon pulled out the cotton and under it lay a gray pouch. She met his gaze, eyes wide. "You look inside the bag," she whispered.

He pulled out the pouch, opened it, and whistled.

"What?" she asked. "What is it?"

He dumped out the contents on the counter. A diamond pendant necklace and two matching earrings caught the light, sending multicolored sparkles in all directions.

"Wow!" Shannon gasped. "No wonder Amanda was so upset. These have got to be worth. . .who knows?"

Her phone trilled in her pocket, and she yanked it out. "Venus again," she mouthed to Glen. "Hey, sweetie. You don't sound so good." She paused and nodded. "Of course you shouldn't come to work tomorrow if you're sick. Promise me you'll get some rest, though." After another pause, Shannon smiled. "That's what I was about to tell you."

Glen listened while Shannon told Venus about the box and its valuable contents. He considered the wisdom of telling anyone about the find until they knew more, but Venus was Shannon's employee.

"I don't know what we're going to do, but you'd better believe the box and this jewelry is going into my safe tonight for protection." Shannon gave a sympathetic hum. "Forget work, you take care, okay?"

She dropped her cell into the pocket of her skirt, and Glen shook his head. "I'm not sure we should keep the box."

"Of course not, but should we call Amanda this late?"

Glen heard the sound of a motorcycle engine, but ignored it. "I need time to think. I don't understand why Amanda didn't just tell us about the jewels." A tickle of dread raised the hairs on the back of his neck.

Shannon looked at the jewels again. "You're right. It doesn't make sense."

"Precisely. Something's impossibly wrong here." He found himself thinking aloud.

"So, what *are* we going to do?" Shannon swiped some strands of hair from her face that had escaped her braid, and he lost his train of thought. He quickly looked away from her and focused on the problem at hand.

"I think we should call the police."

"But what about Amanda?" Shannon asked. "If you don't get it back to her, she said she would never do business with you again."

"Well, I already burned my bridges with her," he said. "I don't think she will bring her business back to me. And I'm quite certain I don't want it, no matter the outcome."

"Well, she said she'd sue us," Shannon said.

"Tell me what you think we should do," he said softly.

The motorcycle engine stopped outside in the alley. Ray had arrived. How did he know Shannon was home?

She shrugged. "I really don't know. We could ask Ray's advice."

That was all Glen wanted to do: ask Ray's advice.

Shannon thumbed through the mail next to the spice box, tossed the flyers aside, and frowned. "I wonder what this is. It's from Mike."

◆

Ray blew through the back door, and Shannon whirled around. Truman, lying on the floor next to the chair, raised his head and wagged his tail.

"I got both your messages," Ray said.

"You're a little late," she murmured as she slipped her finger underneath the flap of a fat white envelope. Maybe Mike had decided she could stay. "We've got the box and the jewels. Now we're trying to figure out what to do. Call Amanda or call the police." She motioned to the spice box on her desk.

"Jewels?" He stalked to the desk, then looked from her to Glen. "Are you kidding me?"

"Messages?" Glen asked at the same time. "You called Ray?"

"Yes, Ray. Jewels. And Glen. I thought we'd need help at the park, but Ray didn't answer his phone. Then I called him again after we recovered the box." Shannon pulled several sheets of paper from the envelope.

"Are you guys crazy? Two amateur detectives." Ray whipped off his leather jacket and tossed it on her chair. "You probably messed up potential evidence."

"What is that?" Glen asked.

Shannon frowned at the letter in her shaky hand and shrugged. "A letter from—"

"I'm referring to Reed here." Glen pointed to Ray, and Shannon lifted her eyes and saw a gun in a holster under Ray's arm.

She inhaled. "Ray? A gun?"

"I have a license to carry," he said.

"Concealed?" Glen continued to stare at Ray. "Who are you?"

"Ray, we need to have a talk. I don't like guns. I want you to take it to your car." Shannon returned her attention to the letter as Ray ignored her instructions and crossed the room to examine the spice box.

She scanned to the bottom of the missive and swallowed hard. "I guess I'm headed back to Walla Walla. Mike isn't re-newing my lease. Not that I expected him to." She sighed. "And Ray, you aren't listening to me."

"I suppose you guys had your fingers all over this thing, right?" Ray said.

"Yes, we did," Glen answered.

Shannon flipped to the attachment. The petition was titled "Renew Our Storefronts," and in the paragraph below, her name was mentioned as one of the store owners who should be evicted. She scanned the signatures. At the top of the list in bold, slanted script was Glen Caldwell. Her heart felt like it froze.

She shook the papers at him. "Glen? You signed this? You

wanted me out of here?"

"Signed what?" He came to stand beside her, and she held the petition up to his face.

Glen took the papers from her hand and began to read.

Ray pulled a cell phone from his pocket and punched in some numbers.

Shannon tore her gaze from Glen and stared at Ray.

"Yeah," he said. "D'Amato? Ray Reed here." He turned his back to them. "Yeah, I'm *that* Reed. The one you had coffee with last night. Listen, I'm pretty sure I've run across some stolen jewels at The Quaint Shop." He paused and listened. "Yes, the same place that was broken into. I need a uniform here with evidence bags." He cocked his head to listen. "Good. See you in a few."

He punched the button to end the conversation, then turned back to face Shannon and Glen. "Someone's right around the corner."

"You're a cop," Glen stated.

"Was," Ray said. "I was."

Shannon backed away. "You? My guitar teacher? The musician." She shook her head. "No, Ray, please tell me—"

"I can explain." Ray eyed her, and she saw the cop, not her good friend. Tears filled her eyes.

She slapped the papers on the desk. "I can't believe it." She pushed her way around Ray.

Glen reached for her hand, but she snatched it away. "And you! You sign this petition to get me thrown out?"

"I didn't know—"

"Move, Glen. I'm leaving."

"Hold up, Shan." Ray stood in front of the door, blocking her exit.

"Don't even start with me. You lied to me." She poked his shoulder with her finger. "I should have known. Remember the other day when I said you were acting like a cop?"

"I didn't lie," Ray said. "I told you I didn't want to discuss my past. And there's a reason—"

"I don't want to hear it." Shannon turned and jabbed a finger into Glen's shoulder. "And furthermore, I don't want to hear anything from you, either. You're both. . .not nice."

Shannon snatched her purse from the floor beside her desk. "I want both of you gone when I get back. Come on, Truman. You're coming with me."

&

Shannon cried as she drove all over the Tri-Cities, from Kennewick to Pasco to Richland and around again. She didn't dare go back to her shop too soon. She wanted to give the police time to arrive and collect the spice box, then time for the two traitors to leave her office. Her curiosity about the spice box and jewels had died in the heartache of discovering how Ray and Glen had misrepresented themselves.

Her stomach growled. On impulse, she pulled into a McDonald's drive-through. "You know what this means, don't you?" she asked Truman.

He wagged his tail.

"It means I'm not as good at reading body language as I thought."

He snuffled her arm, and she stroked his wooly head. Then she sniffled and reached for a napkin from a pile on the floor behind her seat. "I don't even have tissues, Truman. I'm that disorganized. And who knew the two men I trusted most—"

"Welcome to McDonald's."

Shannon swallowed a sob before placing her order. A hamburger for Truman and a fish sandwich with fries for her, along with extra napkins to blow her nose.

She pulled up and paid for the food, ignoring the looks she got from the teen at the window.

Fresh tears threatened as she pulled around, parked, and cut the engine. She unwrapped Truman's burger under his curious gaze, shrugged, and served it to him. "I know. I never eat fast food, and neither do you, but I just don't care tonight."

She took another bite of her sandwich, chewed, and swallowed the food along with a sob. "I still love him—fool that I am. I can't believe he signed that petition and sided with Amanda Franklin, even if he did it weeks ago."

Shannon balled up the trash and stuffed it in the bag. "Let's go home. I've got a lot of work to do. Packing. . .planning. It'll be a good cure for the blues."

The words brought her no comfort. Glen—and Ray. Why hadn't she seen through their facades?

❧

Shannon pulled into the alley behind her shop and parked. "Come on, Truman." Exhaustion made her muscles ache. Her heart ached more. The dog leaped out of the truck and followed her.

Shannon put the key into the lock, shoved the door open, and froze. "What is this?"

Venus, on her knees in front of the safe, looked up. Louis was standing over Venus with a gun pointed at her head. He swung his gun at her. Truman growled and leaped at Louis. He jerked the gun toward the dog and fired.

Truman fell to the floor. Shannon screamed and flew to his side. Blood puddled beneath him. "Truman!"

Still breathing, he looked up into her eyes and whined.

"That dog took a piece of me tonight. What goes around comes around."

"You were at the park tonight?" Shannon's gaze flew to Louis's arm. It was bandaged.

"You shot my dog," she said, anger lowering her voice to a growl that Truman would appreciate.

Louis laughed. "Shut up, drama queen, and get on the floor next to her." He nodded toward Venus.

"Why do you want the spice box now? You can't possibly think you'll get that much money for it from anyone else but Glen." Shannon blinked, wishing she could erase the surreal scene before her eyes.

"I'm here for what's inside the box."

"Venus?" Had Shannon been betrayed one more time?

"He's been stealing from you, Shannon. I found out a couple of days ago. I've been trying to get him to stop. He knew the box was worth a lot of money. He wanted it. And then he heard you tell me about the jewels and he—"

Louis kicked her. "Shut up. Let's keep things simple and nobody has to get hurt."

"I'm sorry, Shannon," Venus whispered.

"Open the safe," Louis said

Venus's hands were shaking. "I can't. I keep getting the combination wrong."

"Try harder." He pointed at the floor. "I told you to sit."

Shannon crossed her arms. "No. And the box isn't in the safe."

"Really? If it's not, I'll shoot you." He waved the gun in her direction. "I'm probably going to shoot you anyway."

Suddenly she was more angry than frightened. "And go to jail for murder?"

Shannon met Venus's mascara-smeared eyes, and a jolt of fury shot through her—a fire like nothing she'd ever felt before.

"I'm sorry," Venus whispered again.

"I told you to shut up!" Louis slapped her across the head with an open palm.

Venus yelped and sobbed.

Truman came to life, barking and struggling to get to his feet.

Louis turned the gun again at Truman. Shannon exploded, leaping toward Louis. She wondered how fast a bullet would kill her.

eighteen

Glen returned to his shop after accompanying Ray to the police station. The police would hold the box and the jewelry until they determined if the jewels were indeed stolen. Now Glen had to make amends to Shannon. He had a plan, but first he had to talk to the landlord.

He pulled into his parking space and heard a muffled explosion like a gunshot or fireworks.

Panicked, he leaped from his BMW. Shannon's truck was parked in its spot. Farther up the alley, he saw Venus's little car parked at an odd angle. Light glowed from the window of Shannon's office, but nowhere else. As he ran toward the back door, he heard Truman bark and Venus yelling.

"Louis, you killed her!" Venus wailed.

"Shut up. Just shut up and get that safe open." The voice was familiar. Similar to the person who had called him.

"Shannon said the box isn't here—"

"I'm sure she lied." Then came the sound of a slap and a scream.

"Louis, why are you doing this?"

Where was Shannon? Glen felt bile in the back of his throat as he pulled out his cell and dialed 911.

Truman barked again. Glen whispered into the phone, "Come, please." Then he left the phone on and stuck it in his pocket.

"I'm going to kill that dog," Louis said.

"Louis, please," Venus begged.

"Open the safe now."

Glen looked up and down the alley for a police car, wishing one was close by. He debated only for a second before he knocked on the door.

Louis murmured something, and Glen pressed himself against the building beside Shannon's door. Holding his breath, he waited till he heard the creak of the rusty door hinges. Slowly Louis stepped outside, gun in hand. Glen shoved the door with all his strength, catching Louis's arm. The gun fell to the ground with a clatter. Glen grabbed it and stepped into the light.

As Louis howled in pain, Glen punched him in the stomach. He went down, and Glen stared into Shannon's office, his gaze searching wildly for her.

"Shannon!" he said. She was slumped on the floor, Venus next to her, and her head was bleeding.

ঽ৯

Shannon slowly opened her eyes and wondered where she was. Then she remembered. She was in Allie's guest room. The events of the night before came flooding back into her mind. Louis, Venus, and the safe. Truman bleeding. Glen bursting into the office and holding her. Had he really been crying? And Ray, all copish, running in with other cops, reading Louis his rights. Venus sobbing while she held Shannon's hand.

She heard a soft knock, and Allie's head appeared around the door. "Are you awake?"

"Yes, barely. My head is killing me."

Allie crossed the room and sat on the side of the bed. "No wonder. That monster Louis walloped you something awful with his gun."

"Thank God the doctor at the Kennewick hospital said I was okay. No major concussion."

"Yes, thank God." Allie stroked a piece of hair out of Shannon's face. "I'm glad you called me and Derrick to come and get you."

"I still can't believe what happened," Shannon said.

Allie shook her head. "Based on what we've heard, the jewels were part of a jewelry heist years ago, but I don't know anything else about that."

"A heist? That sounds sort of old-fashioned."

"It is. It happened a long time ago. It involved the Franklin family."

Shannon didn't care much about the Franklins or the box and jewels at the moment. "How is Venus?"

"They treated her at the hospital for cuts and bruises where that monster hit her."

Shannon felt angry all over again at the memory of Louis slapping Venus. "They didn't arrest her, did they?"

"No. They just took her in for questioning."

Shannon reached for Allie's hand. "Thank you. You and Derrick came to my rescue."

"Not really," Allie said. "You'd already been rescued. By two men who care very much for you."

Shannon's stomach clenched. "I don't want to discuss them."

"You have to. Ray called this morning to see how you are. He explained things. He says the police may need another statement from you."

"I already talked to them. And to him. I don't want to again." Shannon sighed. "You know how I feel about the police."

Allie laughed. "Yes, I know."

"And did he explain to you how I spent months getting to know who I thought he was? Pouring out my heart to him?"

"Perhaps it was a good lesson," Allie said.

Shannon frowned. "What do you mean?"

Allie shrugged. "You're the one who's always seeing meaning behind the way everything happens. And here I am having to explain Ray and Glen to you."

"Sometimes it's harder to see things in your own life," Shannon grumbled.

"Okay, I'll explain. It's easy to judge people by their profession or outward appearance. Ahem. Like all farriers are men—and you know I'm a farrier, and I'm definitely not a man. Or. . .like all cops are *fill-in-the-blank*. All antique dealers with ritzy furniture in their shops are arrogant snobs. But when you get to know the person inside, you find they're not anything like what you assumed."

Once again someone was using her own words against her. She picked at the sheet hem.

"I have another surprise for you in that same vein." Allie's green eyes lit with a smile.

"Should I brace myself?"

"Maybe so. Ray told me he got a call from one Deputy Kroeger." Allie's expression was way too self-satisfied.

"Oh boy, how can that be good news?"

"The deputy wanted to know how you were doing."

"No way." Shannon shook her head. "You've got to be kidding."

"I'm not."

"Why did he call Ray?"

Allie smiled. "Several reasons. After Ray and I talked about the box, he called Deputy Kroeger to talk about it. You know how cops are—"

Shannon snorted.

"No, not like that. I mean they tend to be a close-knit group, even if they don't know each other well. Anyway, he was curious about the box. He'd had suspicions after the break-ins. And then he asked about you."

"I find that hard to believe."

"I'll make it easy for you. The deputy is the reason your parents stopped using drugs. That time he arrested your father, he could have arrested your mother as well. Then you would have ended up in foster care. Kroeger agreed to leave her alone if they promised to stop the drugs. He didn't want to see you harmed in any way. They've kept their word, but he still checks on them from time to time."

Shannon was stunned. "Why did he do it? Couldn't he have gotten in trouble for not arresting my mother like that?"

"I don't know," Allie said. "Maybe. But it seems he saw you

in your bed, gripping your blanket, terrified. That made a huge impact on him."

Shannon tried to wrap her mind around that. "I've been so wrong," she whispered.

"Yeah. And about a lot of things. Like why didn't you tell me how bad things had gotten with the store and the landlord?" Allie pulled her hand from Shannon's. "Derrick could have intervened."

"I guess I didn't realize how bad it was until it was all too late." She took a breath. "Where is Truman?"

"Don't worry, he's downstairs resting. He'll have a scar on his hip, but the bullet only grazed him, thank God."

"Yes. God definitely protected us all." Shannon sat up. "I can't believe I did what I did."

"You mean leaping at an armed man, trying to rescue someone, and being smacked in the head with a gun?"

Shannon smiled. "Well, yeah, if you want to put it that way."

"You were just trying to protect Truman and Venus. That's how you are. You protect your own."

"It's also like me not to think about the consequences of my actions."

"Too true," Allie said. "You've gotten several other calls. Your parents, Pastor Zach and Laurie, Venus, Charlie. . .and did I mention Glen?"

"Glen." Shannon inched her way to the edge of the bed. "Anyway, what's for breakfast?"

"You're avoiding talking about Glen."

"Yes, I am." Shannon shrugged. "French toast?"

"Don't you care that he called?"

Shannon moved until her legs were hanging over the side of the bed. "All I care about right now is eating. So, what are we having?"

"My famous pancakes." Allie held out her hand. "I know. They aren't what you usually eat, but you need some comfort food right now."

"I agree." Shannon slipped out of bed and stretched. "I'm going to shower. I'll be down in ten minutes."

❧

Allie sat across the table from Shannon with baby Natalie against her shoulder. Shannon smiled, watching her best friend gently rub the little one's back. Allie had taken to motherhood in the same manner she'd taken to mothering her nephew, Danny—with her whole heart and soul.

"I think I'm coming back to Walla Walla. I won't fight the eviction."

Allie frowned. "That's not like you. You seem defeated somehow. Perhaps you should wait and make a decision in a few days, after you've returned to Kennewick. And had time to think."

Shannon chewed a bite of pancake slowly. After she swallowed, she met Allie's gaze. "I guess I *feel* defeated. I've realized a lot of things about myself the past few months. . . well, especially the last month. And the biggest one is I'm stubborn and I don't listen to what other people are telling me, even when they mean to help."

Allie didn't disagree. She dropped her gaze and kissed Natalie's little head.

Shannon's throat grew tight. "Glen was right about a lot of things, even though he did go behind my back." She shivered. "To think Glen would side with Amanda against me."

"Shan, you need to hear Glen out," Allie said softly. "I've spoken with him. You must remember Deputy Kroeger. Things aren't always what they appear."

"Hmm." Shannon stuffed more pancake into her mouth. "These are yummy, by the way. Makes me want to go off my regular weird diet more often."

"Maybe it wouldn't hurt you to be more normal," Allie suggested as she stood and put Natalie in her swing. She collected the dishes and began filling the sink with hot water and soap.

"I'm afraid I don't know what normal is."

"No, you wouldn't. Not the way you were raised." Allie laughed. "But your folks are good people. We're praying that they come to the Lord soon."

"He met my mom." In her mind's eye, she saw Glen, acting as though all families lived like hers. "He was out at their trailer."

Allie whirled around. "You took Glen to meet your parents?"

"No!" Shannon shook her head. "He followed me there."

Allie turned back to the dishes. "Why did he follow you there?"

"Because he was worried about me."

"I see." Allie rinsed a plate and set it in the drainer.

"You see what?" Heat burned a path up her face. Didn't Allie grasp how hurt she was seeing Glen's name on that petition?

"Don't get upset. I just want to know if Glen treated you differently after that. Like you were pond scum or something."

"No, but you don't know Glen like I do. He's—he's charming." Shannon closed her eyes. She didn't want to conjure a picture of the tall, handsome Brit wearing a slight smile. "What I mean is, he's too polite to say what he thought." She sighed. This wasn't coming out right.

"Hmm. Charming. Polite. Not to mention kind and concerned. Bad, bad Glen," Allie's voice dripped with sarcastic humor.

"You know what I mean, Allie. Don't make me explain with this pounding headache."

"Fine, but have you given him a chance to explain about the petition or the restore our street committee or whatever it's called?"

"No, but—"

"Ha!" Allie wiped her hands on a dish towel, turned, and leaned against the counter. "It seems to me that you might be just as guilty of judging him as you think he is of you. He didn't know what he was signing. He just did it in a hurry so she'd leave him alone."

"How do you know that?" Shannon asked.

"He told me."

Shannon began to shred her napkin. "I didn't give him a chance to explain." Her shoulders sagged. "There is another good example why I probably shouldn't be in a relationship at all. It's so much work, and I'm so bad at it. I'm a slob, I can't keep books, I eat weird food, I dress funny, and most of my friends are oddballs."

"Excuse me?"

"I said *most*." Shannon sighed. "I just want to come home to Walla Walla and forget everything. I need time to think. Can I stay for a couple more days?"

"Normally I would tell you to stay as long as you wanted, but this time I won't." Allie bit her lip. "You need to go back. The sooner the better. Tomorrow morning? Get things squared away. Even if you have to shut down your store, you still have a decision to make about Glen. And Ray. They both really want to talk to you."

After a long silence, Shannon nodded. "You're right. I'm being childish and stubborn. I'll go back. But no guarantees after that." That's all she could promise right now. Her head throbbed and her body ached, but her heart. . .

She may as well have handed Glen her heart the first time they'd met. How long would it take to get over him? Months? Years?

nineteen

On Wednesday morning, Shannon pulled off the highway to the Tri-Cities, planning her move in her head. She would rent a truck and spend a weekend taking everything from the Tri-Cities store to the shop in Walla Walla. Allie had offered storage in her barn if she needed it.

As she pulled into the alley behind her shop, she saw Glen's car parked there along with Charlie's and Venus's vehicles.

She jammed her truck into PARK, turned it off, and sent up a silent prayer that she wouldn't run into Glen. She couldn't avoid him forever, but she didn't want to face him today.

Glen had challenged who she was. She needed to face her faults. Think about how she impacted other people and not be so determined to do her own thing. Now that she had settled that in her mind, she could begin to change. . .wanted to change. . .with the Lord's help. But she didn't want her motive to be to please Glen. It wasn't fair to him. He needed someone more conventional. Someone more his equal, while she had to define herself on her own terms, not by what Glen or anybody else thought of her.

Shannon exited her truck, went around to the passenger side, and opened the door for Truman. "C'mon, boy." She helped the injured dog down, straining her muscles.

Truman must've sensed her mood. Head hung low, he followed silently.

Shannon stuck the key in her lock, and her heart stilled. After the end of the month, she would never return here again. Turning the knob slowly, she stepped into her office.

A new file cabinet stood against one wall. The floor was clean and had even been waxed. The only thing that remained a mess was the top of her desk. Was Mike already moving someone in? That wasn't legal.

Truman limped past her and curled up next to the leather chair with a sigh.

"Shannon?" Venus shot through the office door and skidded to a stop, her face a question mark.

"Come here," Shannon opened her arms. "I want a hug."

Venus flew across the room and into Shannon's warm hug. "I'm so sorry," she whispered. "You and Truman almost died, and it was all my fault."

"You made a mistake." She pulled away from Venus and put her hands on the girl's shoulders. "You were desperate to be loved, and Louis used that."

"I didn't know what he was going to do." Venus's lower lip trembled. "And he became so mean to me. He threatened me at the end."

"I know that. And that's why you were so stressed out, right?" Venus nodded.

Shannon rubbed her hands up and down the teenager's arms. "I forgive you."

"Thank you so much." A single tear straggled down Venus's cheek. "And you know what's the stupidest thing?"

"What's that?"

"I wanted love so badly, and here was Charlie, right here. He was worried sick about me." Her face colored. "He loves me."

Shannon grinned. "I hoped you'd say that." She waved her hand around the office. "What's going on here? Is someone else moving in already?"

Venus's smile lit her face, and she grabbed Shannon's hand. "No way. Come with me."

She allowed herself to be led into the shop area. In the doorway, Venus dropped her hand, and Shannon stared, her jaw hanging open. This was her store, but everything was organized and tidy.

"Surprise!" Venus squealed.

"What are you doing? Are you organizing so I can pack more easily?"

"Shannon!" Venus clucked her tongue. "Don't you get it?"

"Get what?"

"You're staying."

"No, you don't understand. Mike—"

"Glen arranged it with Mike. Now that Amanda is out of the picture, she isn't running the show anymore."

"Amanda is out of the picture?"

"Wow, where have you been?" Venus giggled. "Oh, that's right. You were in hiding." She inhaled. "Turns out the necklace and earrings were part of a bunch of stuff taken from a jewelry store robbery. Amanda's father owned the store and faked a break-in. He died like five years ago. The necklace and earrings were what was left. They sold off the rest to live high on the hog."

"No wonder Amanda's mother wanted to get rid of them."

"Yeah. She probably felt guilty or something. People sometimes get that way when they think their life is almost over."

Shannon smiled. Sometimes Venus was very insightful.

"Ray said something about the statue of limitations."

"You mean statute?"

"Whatever. Amanda can't be arrested, but she's not rich anymore. Something about freezing. . .freezing. . ."

"Assets?"

Venus smiled. "Yeah."

The front door opened and both of them turned to look. Glen walked in looking tired and decidedly disheveled in jeans and a T-shirt. He had his hands behind his back. Shannon's heart flip-flopped.

"I'm going next door for a minute." Venus zoomed out of the shop.

Glen's smile was hesitant, and he held up a bouquet of daisies he'd been hiding. "Don't leave until I explain." His words came out in a rush. "Please forgive me. I never meant to keep the petition from you. I never actually read it thoroughly. Amanda told me it pertained to upgrading the area. I only signed it to make her leave me alone."

"I know," Shannon said.

"You do?" He approached her with the flowers held out in front of him. "I'm usually so careful about everything, but she was giving me no peace. I just wanted her to get out of my office. And she led me to believe that you knew about the petition and had refused to sign it."

"Wow." Shannon took the flowers and swallowed. "I'm sorry I walked out before you could explain and that I didn't return your calls from Allie's. I made assumptions that weren't right."

"None of us knew the depths of Amanda's wickedness, especially you. You don't have a vicious bone in your body." Glen looked directly into her eyes.

"How did you do this?" Shannon waved an arm around the room. "How did you talk Mike into letting me stay?"

"With Amanda out of the picture, it was easy."

"What about your business?" Shannon asked. "You needed Amanda as a regular client, and you had all that stuff you'd found for her."

Glen smiled. "Turns out I met someone who wants all of that and more. His name is William Shepherd. Ironically, Mike introduced us."

"Wow," Shannon said again. "That's amazing."

Glen put a hand on Shannon's shoulder. "Can we try again?"

"Try again?" She knew what he meant, and she was stalling to try to figure out what to say.

"You and I. Together. See if it'll work out."

"I don't know." Shannon imitated his hesitant smile. "You and I are so different. I can change, but probably never enough to be like you."

He put his other hand on her other shoulder. "Who said I wanted you to be like me? One of me is quite enough, thank you very much."

Her heart lightened, but she had to be sure. "We'd be like the *Odd Couple*."

Venus entered the shop from the back.

"I always liked that old movie." Glen's eyes crinkled in a smile. "Now, can you please forgive me for being bossy?"

"Of course." Shannon stepped closer to Glen. "I'm sorry I never listened or asked for your help, even when I knew you were right. I was embarrassed, I guess. And stubborn."

He came closer, and she couldn't resist. She flung her arms around his neck, and Glen kissed her soundly.

Venus giggled and applauded, then said, "I wondered when you guys would stop yakking long enough to kiss."

twenty

Wednesday night, Ray was slouched in Shannon's leather chair, wooden chopsticks stuck in a white box of Chinese food. "That was good." He put the empty container on the floor.

"Yes." Shannon placed her half-eaten food on her desk. "Dinner was my apology offering."

"And so it should be. You were cruel to me."

Shannon smiled. "You could at least be a little more humble."

He splayed his hand on his chest. "I am your humble servant."

She laughed. "Right. So will you tell me more about your job?"

His smile faded, and he took a deep breath. "Really, you already know the most important things. My spiritual and emotional struggles. Right now, you can just pray for me. I'm deciding whether or not I want to go back into law enforcement." He leaned forward. "So, you've accepted the fact that I'm part of the 'establishment'?"

She nodded. "Yes. And I was so wrong. Me, who prided herself in accepting everyone. I'm really, really sorry."

He smiled and kicked her foot gently with his. "Shan, you're fine. We're all growing in the Lord, and sometimes it's messy."

"Well, I prided myself in accepting everyone, but I wasn't an 'equal opportunity' accepter."

He laughed. "Welcome to the human race. You're not perfect. And we don't need to discuss it again. You and I are fine."

"Good," she said.

"So, what did Caldwell get for his apology offering?"

Shannon blushed. "A kiss."

"I hope he got more than only one after what you put the poor man through."

"Ray!" Shannon's face heated.

"I saw him after you were taken to the hospital. He was a wreck."

Shannon couldn't speak for the emotion that overcame her.

"So," Ray said. "I suppose next you're going to want all the gory details?"

"Yes. The spice box, jewels, the break-ins, and everything."

"I'll tell you what I can." He paused. "You know where the jewels came from and why Amanda wanted them back so badly, right?"

"Yes."

"The DA is figuring things out now. Amanda did not commit insurance fraud. Her father did, years and years ago, but she knew about it and used the money. Statute of limitations is up, but the insurance company will demand restitution. She will also be charged with breaking and entering your office on Sunday morning."

Shannon sucked in a breath. "Amanda did that?"

"Yeah." Ray huffed out a breath. "No matter what, her reputation is shot."

Shannon felt a deep sense of grief. "I didn't like her much, but I would never wish anything like this on anybody."

"I know, but when people break the law, they have to be punished."

"Yes, I know, Mr. Cop." Shannon smiled at him.

He gave her a wink. "And Louis is already in jail. Judge denied him bail. Charged with assault with a deadly weapon, robbery, breaking and entering, to name a few."

"So he is the one who broke into the homes?"

"You got that right."

"Thank you for not involving Venus."

Ray shrugged. "That was partially as a result of Glen's and my intervention at the scene. But she really wasn't guilty of anything but stupidity. She had no clue what Louis was up to until that Monday. And he threatened her if she told."

"So that's why she left work early?"

"Yep. He was afraid she'd cave and tell you. He planned to hit Glen and run away with the box *and* the money. He knew the box was worth money, which was why he originally went after it—apparently Venus exaggerated its worth. But he had no idea the box held anything valuable until you told Venus that night."

Shannon rubbed her arms with her hands. "The Lord was certainly protecting all of us through this."

"Yes, He was." Ray smiled and stood. "And now I must leave, but I've made sure you won't be left alone." He glanced at his watch. "Five, four, three, two. . ."

Someone rapped on the door. Shannon jumped up and opened it. "Glen!"

Ray laughed. "I invited him. It seems a shame for you two to be apart your first evening back."

Glen grinned and reached for her hand. She watched as Ray jogged outside with a backward wave. When he mounted his bike, Glen reached out, pushed the door shut, and pulled her into his arms.

epilogue

With Truman close on her heels, Shannon scurried from her truck to the back door of The Quaint Shop, hauling her backpack, a bag of spring decorations for the store, and her purse.

She caught a glimpse of Venus's car, unlocked the back door, and strode through her office to the showroom. "Venus?" she yelled. "Why are you still here?"

"Shannon! You're back." Venus popped up from behind the counter, breathless. "I have a date with Charlie, and he's just closing up next door, so I waited."

Venus stepped around the counter and hugged her. "I missed you a whole lot."

"I missed you, too." Shannon let go of Venus, shoved aside a box, and dropped her backpack on the floor. "I brought pictures of Natalie's birthday party. She's a little charmer." Shannon stretched. "I feel so relaxed."

Venus crossed her arms and sighed. "I'll bet you had so much fun with Allie that you wished you could be back in Walla Walla."

"I had fun, but being there for a week confirmed for me that this is my home." She inhaled the scent of her store and realized how true her words felt. She was truly home.

"I'm glad," Venus said. "And I'm sure Glen will be glad you feel that way, too. Did you miss him? Has he called you from London? Is his brother's wife okay?"

"Yes, I miss him. And I hear from him every day. Melissa is making a full recovery from surgery, and the doctors say the cancer is in remission. Glen's having an awesome time with his family. I can't wait until he comes back. Three weeks is a long time not to see him." That was putting it mildly. She wanted nothing more than to be held tightly in his arms.

Venus's cell phone buzzed. "I've got a text message. One sec." While she punched quickly on the phone buttons, Shannon reached under the counter for her notebook containing sales records. She still hadn't succumbed to a computerized record-keeping system, although Glen was slowly convincing her that it would be worthwhile.

Venus shoved her phone into her pocket, then pushed the box on the counter toward her. "This came for you, Shan."

"Okay." Shannon acknowledged the box with a nod. "How is Charlie doing holding down the fort for Glen? It's a good thing this was spring break, huh?"

"Charlie is doing great!" Venus said with pride in her voice. She patted the carton. "Aren't you going to open this?"

After noting that sales had been brisk, Shannon slipped the notebook back under the counter and eyed the package. "It looks like the stationery and business cards and other office supplies I ordered." She yawned. "I'm tired. It can wait until tomorrow."

"But there's no return address on it," Venus said. "Doesn't that make you wonder?"

Shannon pulled the box toward her. "You're right. No return address. That's weird. Maybe it fell off. Could be a bomb."

"That's not funny," Venus said.

Shannon laughed. "Like I'm that important, right?" She pulled at the packing tape, growing more curious. "If it's the office stuff, they used a lot of unnecessary tape. Can you hand me a pair of scissors?"

Venus reached underneath the counter and rummaged around, then stood, triumphant, waving a pair. "Here you go."

The sleigh bells rang on the front door. Shannon looked up as Charlie strolled in.

"Hi, Charlie," Shannon said as she sliced through the tape across the top of the box. "You're just in time to be blown up."

"Hi, Shannon. Um, what?" When he reached them, Venus stepped into his open arms and hugged him tight.

"Kidding. I've got an unidentified package here addressed to me." Shannon looked up. "It's good to see you. Do you miss Glen as much as I do?"

Charlie laughed and draped his arm around Venus's shoulders. "I doubt it. I'm not going out with him. We don't kiss each other."

The reminder of Glen's kisses made Shannon blush. Venus laughed.."You give yourself away."

"Knock, knock, anybody here?"

Shannon twirled around to see Ray enter the shop from her office, smiling broadly. "Howdy, stranger. Missed you, girl."

"Ray. . ." Her heart lifted, and she felt an accompanying pang of sadness. "So, copper, are you still packing to leave town and return to your previous profession with the establishment, or have you changed your mind and decided to continue your music career?"

He crossed the room with long strides and pulled her into a hug. "Yes, I'm still packing to leave. I've decided to return to the *establishment*. Then in my dotage I'll have a good pension and will be able to once again pursue my musical career." He nodded at Venus and Charlie, then looked at the box. "What's in there?"

"It's doubtful we'll ever find out," Venus said. "She keeps getting interrupted. But so far it's either stationery or a bomb."

Charlie pushed at the box. "I'm guessing it's books."

Shannon laughed. "Ray, you want to venture an opinion?"

"Nope. Just open the box. I only believe what I see."

She pulled up the flaps and looked inside. "Lots of packing material." She pulled out a block of blown-in foam and dropped it on the counter. "Hmmm. I think I'll need help with this."

Venus helped her slide out a bubble-wrapped parcel.

"Listen, while you do that, I have something for you," Ray said. "I'll be right back."

"Okay." Shannon paid him little attention as he disappeared into her office.

Venus peeled off the wrapping with her, and Shannon glimpsed the contents and sucked in a breath.

"It's a spice box," Venus said.

Shannon shook her head. "There's been a mistake. I didn't order this."

"Maybe it belongs to Glen," Charlie said.

She heard Ray come back into the store, but didn't look up. Running her fingers across the fine grain wood, she whistled. "It's a beauty."

"Even if it was delivered here accidentally," Charlie said, "I don't think Mr. Caldwell would mind if you looked inside it."

Shannon examined again the label on the box. "It's addressed to me. How can it be an accident?"

"There's been no accident."

Shannon's heart stopped at the sound of the familiar British accent. She looked up. Ray stepped aside revealing Glen standing behind him.

"Here's your surprise." Ray grinned broadly and high-fived Glen.

"You're home early." Shannon slipped out from behind the counter and had to stop, her legs suddenly weak.

Glen's long strides quickly covered the distance between them. He reached her, took her hands in his, and kissed her gently. "You have no idea how much I've missed you."

"I think I do," she whispered.

"What about this?" Venus pointed at the spice box.

"Hmmm." Glen stepped away from Shannon and examined the box. "I see your store has once again been mistaken for mine."

Ray, Venus, and Charlie laughed.

"Very funny, everyone." Shannon eyed each of them. "Coconspirators, I assume?"

"Good guess, Sherlock," Ray said.

Glen draped his arm around her shoulders and kissed her cheek. She faced him for a proper kiss, but Venus cleared her throat.

"Enough smooching right now. I'm curious." Venus hovered close by.

"Do you think this box has a secret compartment?" Shannon couldn't resist pulling open the bottom drawer.

"It's likely," Glen said. "Go on, check it out."

"This box is lovely," Shannon said as she searched for the hidden button.

"Lovely," Glen said, looking into her eyes.

Warmth washed over her, and she gave Glen a smile. "I found the secret button!" She released the back and turned it around.

He moved so close to her she could feel the warmth of his breath on her cheek. If she turned even a fraction, their lips would meet in a kiss. How she longed for his kiss, to be in his arms again. . . .

Shannon slid the wooden back down, pulled out the drawer divide, and found the hidden compartment.

"I wonder if jewels are stashed in this one," Charlie joked.

Shannon's curiosity got the best of her. She pulled open the drawer and gasped. "There—there's a ring in here in a blue velvet holder."

"Not more stolen jewels, I hope." Shaking his head, Ray blew out a breath. "There's been too much crime and mayhem around here. I need to return to police work to escape."

Charlie and Venus laughed.

"Let's have a look." Glen picked up the ring. "It's a yellow and white diamond daisy." He held it out so Shannon could see it.

"A daisy," she whispered, her heart beating fast. Was it

possible? "I've never seen a ring this beautiful in all my life."

Glen dropped to one knee in front of her. "You, Shannon O'Brien, have captured my heart and soul and mind."

Looking down at the man she loved with all her heart, tears of joy trickled from her eyes. "Glen, I—I. . ." Aware that her three friends were in the room, the words wouldn't come.

"They already know we're in love." Glen took her hand and looked up into her eyes. "Shannon O'Brien, will you marry me?"

She dropped to her knees in front of him. "Yes, yes, yes."

Glen slipped the ring on her finger, smiling. "I love you." He yanked her into his arms and kissed her soundly.

Ray whistled. "Whoa. And I thought the Brits were cold. I'm feelin' the heat from here."

Charlie and Venus laughed.

Glen helped Shannon to her feet. "Folks, let me present my fiancée and best friend, Shannon O'Brien."

Ray shook Glen's hand.

"Hey," Venus said. "It all started and finished with a box."

A Letter To Our Readers

Dear Reader:

In order that we might better contribute to your reading enjoyment, we would appreciate your taking a few minutes to respond to the following questions. We welcome your comments and read each form and letter we receive. When completed, please return to the following:

Fiction Editor
Heartsong Presents
PO Box 719
Uhrichsville, Ohio 44683

1. Did you enjoy reading *Boxed into Love* by Candice Speare and Nancy Toback?
   - ❏ Very much! I would like to see more books by this author!
   - ❏ Moderately. I would have enjoyed it more if

   _____

   _____

   _____

2. Are you a member of **Heartsong Presents**? ❏ Yes ❏ No
   If no, where did you purchase this book? _____

   _____

3. How would you rate, on a scale from 1 (poor) to 5 (superior), the cover design? _____

4. On a scale from 1 (poor) to 10 (superior), please rate the following elements.

   _____ Heroine   _____ Plot
   _____ Hero   _____ Inspirational theme
   _____ Setting   _____ Secondary characters

5. These characters were special because? _____

_____

_____

6. How has this book inspired your life? _____

_____

_____

7. What settings would you like to see covered in future
   Heartsong Presents books? _____

_____

_____

8. What are some inspirational themes you would like to see
   treated in future books? _____

_____

_____

9. Would you be interested in reading other **Heartsong
   Presents** titles? ☐ Yes ☐ No

10. Please check your age range:
    ☐ Under 18   ☐ 18-24
    ☐ 25-34   ☐ 35-45
    ☐ 46-55   ☐ Over 55

Name _____

Occupation _____

Address _____

City, State, Zip _____

E-mail _____

Heartsong ❤

Any 12 Heartsong Presents titles for only $27.00*

CONTEMPORARY ROMANCE IS CHEAPER BY THE DOZEN!

Buy any assortment of twelve *Heartsong Presents* titles and save 25% off the already discounted price of $2.97 each!

HEARTSONG PRESENTS TITLES AVAILABLE NOW:

Presents